"Puerto Rican hot chocolate," she said, taking her seat again.

"Maybe the sugar will perk you up."

"You're worried about me falling asleep at the wheel. No one's worried about me in a very long time."

"In my family, worrying is an Olympic sport, so if you ever need someone to worry about you, feel free to borrow any of us."

He smiled into his cup. "I appreciate the offer."

If the chocolate had been bliss, the cake was pure decadence. "This tres leches is wrecking me."

Her proud smile nearly provoked a desire to cast the cake aside and kiss her. "It's my Saturday Special. I offer it together with flan and crème brûlée. Do you want to try them, also?"

"No, it's too much. Save it for next time." He paused, steeling himself. "That is, if next time is okay with you."

"I wasn't really looking for anything tonight."

"Neither was I. But here we are."

Dear Reader,

When I found out that I had been awarded Harlequin's 2020 Romance Includes You Mentorship, the news left me speechless. And for a person who loves to talk as much as I do, that's saying something.

I got to work with a wonderful editor, Charles Griemsman, who guided me through all the steps of bringing a book from manuscript to publication. That singular access has made all the difference in developing me as a writer and I am forever grateful to Charles and to Harlequin for the opportunity.

The journey from sneaking Harlequin romances from my mother's collection as a young girl to publishing my debut novel with the Harlequin Special Edition line is one I could never have predicted. Sometimes I still can't believe it, though the book in your hands is proof that it must have happened, right?

Thank you for choosing to read *A Delicious Dilemma*. I can't wait for you to meet Val Navarro. Val defines herself in relation to her family, her business and her connection to the fictional working-class community of East Ward, New Jersey. Just like most of us, she wears multiple hats—business owner, community leader, chef, daughter, sister—and manages to juggle them all without dropping anything. And just like us, she's not afraid to take on anyone who threatens the things that she loves.

I'd love to hear from you! Head over to www.serataino.com and sign up for my newsletter. While you're at it, follow me on social media. Instagram, Twitter and Facebook are where I share the most information about my writing and upcoming events. Can't wait to chat it up with you!

Sera

A Delicious Dilemma

SERA TAÍNO

HARLEQUIN
SPECIAL
EDITION

HARLEQUIN®
SPECIAL
EDITION™

Recycling programs
for this product may
not exist in your area.

ISBN-13: 978-1-335-40806-8

A Delicious Dilemma

Copyright © 2021 by Sera Taíno

For questions and comments about the quality of this book,
please contact us at CustomerService@Harlequin.com.

Harlequin Enterprises ULC
22 Adelaide St. West, 40th Floor
Toronto, Ontario M5H 4E3, Canada
www.Harlequin.com

Printed in U.S.A.

Sera Taíno writes Latinx romances exploring love in the context of family and community. She is the 2019–2020 recipient of the Harlequin Romance Includes You Mentorship, resulting in the publication of her debut contemporary romance, *A Delicious Dilemma*. When she's not writing, she can be found teaching her high school literature class, crafting, and wrangling her husband and two children.

Visit the Author Profile page at Harlequin.com.

To my husband,
who has always encouraged me to chase my dreams.

And to my mother.
I think she would have liked this one.

Chapter One

"I hold you personally responsible for my discomfort," Val complained as she scrambled out of her cousin Olivia's Jeep. The relentless percussion from Aguardiente Lounge assailed her from across the parking lot, bringing with it a flicker of anxiety that she tried to ignore. "My fingers are still sore from the manicure."

Olivia rounded the fender, her weight balanced on the balls of her feet. A balmy, spring breeze from the Hudson blew cool and insistent, ruffling their outfits, which were skimpier than what Val was used to. "Do you know how hard it was to get an appointment at the salon on a Friday night? It wouldn't have taken so long if you'd kept up with your nails." She paused, unhooking the heel of her thigh-high boot from where it had become wedged in the pavement. "You'd think Rosario would spend a little money to repave the parking lot."

Val made a face. "Jesus, they should award degrees in complaining, because you'd have a PhD."

"Look who's talking, Darth Cupcake," Olivia retorted, using the nickname she'd christened Val with ever since they'd nearly burned down the family restaurant as kids, trying to make cupcakes from scratch. "Get a little polish on your nails and you act like you got tortured by the Spanish Inquisition."

"I'm not used to having my cuticles poked at, okay?" Val walked alongside Olivia, who was watching the ground for more crevices as Val tugged at the too-short, black-and-silver romper Olivia had loaned her. Val would never give her cousin the satisfaction of knowing she found the outfit pretty in a Kardashian sort of way, with its tiny designs woven onto a lace overlay against a satin camisole. A belt of the same satiny material tied into a bow at the waist, followed by shorts that were barely long enough to cover Val's thighs. The soft ivory accents complemented her deep, olive-brown complexion.

They entered the foyer of Aguardiente Lounge, where Caio, the host on duty, waved them in.

"*Oye*, look who's here!" He bent his tall, wide frame to allow Val to kiss him on his cheek, the scruff of his dark goatee scraping against her skin.

"Olivia," he said when he straightened. "How'd you get her to come out?"

"She dragged me kicking and screaming," Val answered, smiling warmly at him.

"She's not even exaggerating." Olivia jabbed her thumb at Val. "She was still swearing at me as we were coming up from the parking lot."

"I don't swear. That's all you."

"Like hell you don't," Olivia retorted.

Caio laughed at them both. "You two don't change, like two *perritas* always barking at each other. You having dinner or just going straight to the back?"

"No dinner tonight," Olivia answered.

"I'll let you in without the cover. It's gonna be packed anyway."

"Ooh, your stingy cousin isn't going to pitch a fit?" Olivia asked.

"You gonna tell her?" He hugged them both, practically lifting Val off the ground. "It's good to see you, mama. I'm glad you didn't let that guy keep you down."

Val's stomach knotted at the mention of her ex. Luke had been a roller-coaster ride, with his on-again/off-again commitment to her, his betrayal and public humiliation. It would be a lie to say she didn't miss the intimacy of having a steady boyfriend. The late Sunday mornings spent in bed, or having a ready partner to dance with when she craved a night out. But the trade-off—her peace of mind for the exhausting vigilance required to keep Luke's attention from wandering off—was more than she was willing to make again. She'd wasted two years on that man and spent an additional eight months recovering after she'd found out she was nothing more than his side piece. In public. Right here, of all places. Practically in her *house*. No wonder she'd stayed away until tonight.

She patted Caio's shoulder. "He did for a little while, but it's all good now."

"Hope so. You didn't deserve the way he did you." He stepped aside. "Have a good time tonight."

They bypassed the restaurant, heading toward the club proper. The outdoor patio area looked out over a promontory, yielding a view of Riverside Park across the river in Manhattan. Here, the music was a rhythmic backdrop that still permitted conversation. Wooden beams crisscrossed overhead, while the glass walls opened to allow the river air to float in on warmer nights like tonight.

Val and Olivia glided through different groups of people. Val recognized almost everyone in the club, either because she'd gone to school with them, hosted them at the community meetings or served them at Navarro's Family Restaurant, which she owned together with her father.

Val slowed her approach to the dance floor as her heart rate soared. "I'm so freaked out."

Olivia put an arm around Val's shoulder and

squeezed. "You'll get your groove back. Give yourself a chance."

Olivia got on Val's last nerve most of the time, but Val could count on her cousin to have her back. She always could, ever since they were little kids, running amok in the neighborhood. Val couldn't say that about many people. She'd trusted Luke, thought he might have her back, as well. But it had been a lie, and she'd learned her lesson too well: you couldn't let people get that deep under your skin. If you did, you were giving them the power to destroy you.

Val swallowed her anxiety. She could do this. She could enjoy herself here, even after everything that had happened. Clutching at the rosary she always wore, the one that had belonged to her late mother, she closed her eyes and let the beat of a slow bachata settle into her bones. As she swayed, her heart relented, beating as if in time with the music. She missed this. It had been ages since she danced, and the last time had been with Luke.

She needed to stop thinking about that faithless jerk. Not tonight. Tonight belonged to her.

She closed her eyes, immersing herself in the music, until someone tapped her on the shoulder. She opened her eyes to Rosario Villanueva, the owner of Aguardiente Lounge. She was in her late forties, but she wore her short leather skirt, tiny tank top and boots like a rock star.

She gave both Val and Olivia a kiss on the cheek in greeting, and the three of them made their way to the bar. Olivia leaned into Rosario's shoulder, whispering loudly, "I'm on a mission."

Rosario's perfectly shaped eyebrows arched all the way to her hairline. "Really? What do you have in mind, *traviesa*?"

"Val needs to break her dry spell tonight."

Rosario erupted into laughter while Val glared at Olivia. Loyal or not, sometimes it surprised her the amount of time she spent with someone who tempted her to commit murder.

"Don't give me that stink eye," Olivia continued. "I'm meeting Aleysha tonight, so you're going to have to find your own entertainment."

"Traitor," Val shot back, all the while finding comfort in the familiarity of their verbal sparring. "You're abandoning me for your girlfriend?"

"It's not abandonment." Olivia shrugged, her straight black bob bouncing in time with the motion. "Think of it as incentivizing you."

Rosario was breathless with laugher. "I've missed you two. You don't need nobody but yourselves to have a good time." She turned to the bartender, who was doing her best to stifle her own giggles. "Give the girls a free round on me. Welcome back, Val," she said, giving her another kiss before floating away to circulate among the other patrons.

"Guess she's not that cheap, after all," Val admonished Olivia.

"Oh, please, the markup on these drinks is ridiculous." Olivia drummed her nails on the bar counter. "Rum punch, please."

Val threw up her hands in defeat. "I can't go anywhere with you." She pretended to scan the crowd, putting distance between herself and the truth of Olivia's teasing words. It had been a long time, but she'd needed the break to recover from her torn-up heart and bruised ego.

Val took a sip of her *añejo*, listening to the beats of a reggaetón mash-up as it boomed through the room. People made their way to the dance platform, dappled in colors from the strobe lights. Val loved the way the music blasted through her body, the reverberations of the pumping bass through her bones; it had been too long since she'd felt this loose.

Olivia, who had stopped to talk to people she knew, grabbed Val by the hand and pulled her onto the dance floor.

"I also forgot how much fun dancing could be," Val shouted.

"Yeah, that Luke did a number on you," Olivia shouted back.

Val waved her hands, indicating she didn't want to talk about Luke or anyone else. She just wanted to enjoy the music, let her mind grow empty of everything except the lyrics and the beat. Reggaetón was a gift to someone like her—US born but every bit as Puerto Rican as a transplant could be without having lived on the island. It was the soundtrack of the *vaivén*, or the back-and-forth movement that characterized the migration of people going from the mainland to the island and back again.

Val danced until the song changed. Olivia's face split into an uncharacteristically dazzling smile at her girlfriend's arrival. Aleysha's smooth, dark skin contrasted sharply with light brown eyes the color of burnished bronze that were shocking even from a distance.

Aleysha raced over to them, giving Val a glossy, messy kiss on her cheek before flinging her arms around Olivia. "Why didn't you text me when you got here?"

Olivia shrugged. "I figured you'd be late, like always, so why stress you?"

"You're one to talk. Let's go sit with Malena." She gave Val a wink. "She's been seeing this one guy and he brought a friend of his."

Ugh, not a spontaneous blind date. That was the last thing she needed tonight. But of course, before she could say no, Olivia spoke for her. "Why not?"

"I'm not really—" Val started but Aleysha put a hand on her shoulder.

"We're just hanging out. No pressure, okay?"

She just wanted to dance, maybe catch a buzz and go home in peace. But Olivia and Aleysha were wrapped up in each other, so Val had no choice but to follow them. At the far end of the patio, she recognized Malena, who often stopped into her family's restaurant for a late lunch. She sold real estate in one of the smaller boutique agencies in Wagner Financial Place. Malena was leaning into a good-looking man she introduced as Étienne, who said his name with a voluptuous, Creole accent.

At the end of the table, almost in his own orbit, sat Étienne's friend.

"And this is Philip," Aleysha said.

He was whispering something to Étienne, initially unaware of her, but when he turned, the overhead lights flashed, illuminating the most striking blue eyes she'd ever seen. They reminded her of the Caribbean lapping at the beaches of Ponce, where her family used to vacation when she was a child. Music skipped through the space between them before passing her by. How long had she been staring at him. A few seconds? Minutes?

She gave him a cursory wave, determined to cover her dazed reaction before taking the seat next to Olivia. He had the kind of face that was just shy of being too good-looking and it kept dragging at her attention. Through sheer force of will, she fixed her gaze on her cousin to tame her wayward eyes, focusing intensely on her conversation without really processing the meaning of her words. Maybe if she ignored him, he'd forget she was there.

But she didn't have that kind of luck. He slid into the chair next to her and cleared his throat.

"You seem to really enjoy dancing," he said.

That meant he'd been watching her. "I wouldn't do it otherwise," she snapped. His surprised expression forced her to take a deep breath and calm down. No sense being rude to the guy. "My family," she began more slowly. "We dance all the time."

She tried not to actually look at him, but damn, it was hard. He was a study in symmetry but his eyes were kind and approachable, nullifying the aloofness of his good looks.

"Festive group." He recovered, giving her a smile, which improved his already-exceptional features.

She picked up a coaster, toying with it. "Yep, you name it, we dance to it. Birthdays, holidays, first tooth, first traffic ticket…"

His laughter prickled at her skin. Val's eyes slid to where the others in her group conversed, but they were oblivious to the way the air had galvanized around her.

"My family doesn't dance. At all." He said the last part with a cutting sweep of his hand. "I have known my mother to sway a little on her feet at cocktail parties. But that could easily be because of the martinis."

A laugh bubbled unbidden from her. She tried to stop herself. Cocktail parties? Did people actually throw those outside of '80s TV shows? The sound caught Olivia's attention, and she raised an eyebrow in response. Val bit back her laughter. She was not going to give Olivia a reason to tease her.

Étienne had already pulled Malena out of her chair, and was dancing a slow grind against her despite the energetic beat. Olivia returned to her conversation with Aleysha, their heads so close, their cheeks were practically smashed together.

"Drink?" Philip asked as a server approached. She recognized her as Gloria, one of Rosario's infinite number of cousins, just as she scooped Val into a welcoming hug.

"Val!" Gloria released her. "Oh, my God, girl, it's about time you showed your face. It's been forever."

"Yeah, well…"

Gloria took her hand, sliding her thumb over the glossy nude color of Val's nails, and the tiny diamond twinkling on the nail of her ring finger. "Look at those nails. They won't last a week in the restaurant. Want a refill?"

"*Añejo*, if you don't mind," Val answered.

Gloria gave her a thumbs-up before turning to Philip, who handed her his empty beer bottle, an amused expression on his face.

"So, it's been a while for you, too?" he asked when Gloria walked away.

"A while?"

"Since you've been out. The waitress. She said it had been forever since she'd seen you."

Val debated on what to say, then opted for the truth. She'd been lied to so many times, she couldn't stand the idea of doing that to anyone else.

"I was dating someone. After we broke up, I stayed away for a while." She avoided his gaze, tearing bits off the now-frayed coaster.

"Sounds like you needed to take care of yourself."

She froze in her coaster abuse. "That's what I keep telling everyone. You'd think people who'd known me all my life wouldn't feel the need to badger me about it," she murmured mostly to herself.

He stared at her a beat too long and it occurred to her that she wasn't making any sense. "I'm sorry. I'm being a Debbie Downer. What about you? What's your tale of woe?"

He chuckled, taking a swig of his beer before pointing toward the dancers. "I'm not interesting enough to have a tale of woe. You see that maniac over there, draped over Malena like a mink coat?"

Val followed his line of vision to where Étienne was dancing provocatively with Malena.

"He's my best friend. And he threatened me if I didn't go out with him tonight."

"Because?"

"Because…" He shook his head. "Because I'm a workaholic and I'd still be in the office if he hadn't rescued me."

"You're right. My tale of woe is much more interesting than yours."

The smile he gave her made her knees weak. "What would you have done if you'd stayed home?"

Val thought wistfully of her Yoda pajamas, her copy of a *Star Wars* novel and three episodes of *The Great British Bake Off* on her queue. "Probably catch up on my *Star Wars* novel."

"Star Wars," he said, his excitement palpable. "Too bad Disney threw out the Expanded Universe."

Val's eyes grew wide, and she forgot herself completely. "They had to! The Expanded Universe had become such a sprawling mess. It wasn't internally consistent any longer."

Philip's eyes flicked to her lips before returning to hold her gaze. His geek-out was real but something in that glance stole her breath. The sea roared back to her consciousness, and she looked away before it pulled her into its endless blue.

"The Legends are sacred. The least they could have done was keep the major arcs and change the inconsistencies." He actually sniffed in indignation and it was quite possibly the cutest thing she'd ever seen.

She raised her glass. "Maybe if they had, the new trilogy would have been different. Instead, we got… what we got."

"I'll toast to that." Philip clinked his bottle against her drink. Olivia always teased Val for her little obsessions. But she couldn't believe it. There was no way this gorgeous guy could have that in common with her.

Val's nerves quieted to a low hum, and she gave herself permission to relax, taking refuge in the safety of a conversation based purely on their mutual love of *Star Wars*. Olivia and Aleysha had long melted onto the dance floor, while Étienne and Malena went AWOL for the better part of an hour. Philip's hands claimed her attention. Strong and elegant, they were also soft, like a pianist's.

He finished off his beer. "So, what's this about a restaurant?" he asked. "Is that where you work?"

"I own it together with my father. It's not too far from here."

An expression flickered across his face and disappeared when he smiled again. "What's on the menu?"

"Mostly Puerto Rican cuisine, with some variations. We serve breakfast and lunch, though I've been toying with introducing a dinner menu on the weekends. I'm still up in the air on that one because I like having a life."

"Are you the main cook, as well?"

"Chef," she corrected. "I'm trained. Got a degree and everything to show for it."

Philip's surprise didn't annoy her, laced as it was with something that looked like admiration.

"Well, come on. Your turn." She tapped his forearm, which was remarkably hard. She wanted to do it again, but that would just be weird.

Philip shifted in his chair, glancing around him before looking at Val. "I work in real estate."

Something about the way he hesitated made Val pay attention. "You make it sound like you're some secret agent."

"Again, I'm really not that interesting."

"It's a good time to be a real estate agent in East Ward ever since they built that light-rail station." Val pulled a face, gathering up her abandoned coaster and recommencing her torture of it.

"You don't like that?"

"How can I? Everyone I know has been getting letters from developers wanting to buy their properties, including our building."

Philip shifted again. "You could just not sell the property."

"Problem is, I don't own the building my restaurant occupies. And the last building that was bought, they started forcing out tenants because they couldn't afford the new rents."

Philip rolled his shoulders before reaching for his empty beer bottle, then setting it down again. "I thought… I mean I heard through the grapevine that it was a straight renovation project, which is good for the city, right?"

Val gave him her best "Don't be an idiot" look. "Making improvements in itself is not necessarily a bad thing. But the company buying everything up, Wagner Developments, has been super resistant to negotiating with the community. Things will only get worse once they finalize the project for the pencil factory complex they bought on the waterfront." She swept her hands out to indicate their surroundings. "Did you know this building used to be abandoned?"

"No." He glanced around him, nodding in what looked like approval.

"Rosario, the owner, has always lived in East Ward. She got a small business loan from a fund that helped members of the community improve their own spaces. And that's what she did." Val swept her hand to indicate the veranda, with its sleek trimmings and cool river wind. "Then they discontinued the program."

"You know a lot about this," Philip half asked, half stated.

"I should. I'm cofounder of the East Ward Fair Housing Coalition, or EWFHC. If some franchise had leased this space from Wagner Developments, I guarantee we would be having a very different experience right now."

Val crossed her arms, expecting him to mansplain to her all the ways she was wrong. She was used to it and she was ready. But he didn't. He trained those ridiculous blue eyes on her instead, and said, "It'd still be a good one if you were a part of it."

Val ignored the flush of pleasure at his words. She wanted to explain how worried she was that the owners of her building might give in and sell it. How important her restaurant was to her and her family. How afraid she was of losing everything. But Étienne materialized beside them, putting an end to any chance of saying these things. He bowed dramatically before Val.

"May I borrow this young man for a moment? I have a transportation issue to resolve."

Philip locked eyes with Val. "You aren't leaving yet, are you?"

She should, since she'd stayed longer than she'd intended. But Philip had also been fun and easy to speak to and not exactly hard on the eyes. "Actually, yes, but I guess I can wait a few minutes."

He lifted his hand as if to touch her face, but quickly dropped it, a move that blew all the thoughts out of her mind. "Be right back." Philip walked off with Étienne, leaving Val to stare dumbly after him. Olivia slid into the chair he vacated, leaning shoulder to shoulder into Val.

"You okay, Darth Cupcake?"

Luckily, the lights were dim enough to hide the full body flush that overheated her. "I'm good." Then she added lamely, "Nice guy."

"Nice guy, my left ass cheek. Your eyes are so bright, you look like you smoked a bong."

Thank God for Olivia. She was like the human version of a bucket of ice. "I don't smoke, so how would you know what I look like?"

"Not the point. Aleysha!" she called. "Come here. Who is this guy?"

Aleysha leaned in close, toying with the blunt end of Olivia's bangs. "You mean, where has Étienne been hiding him? I just met him, too."

Olivia made a noncommittal sound. "Malena told me he's Étienne's best friend. Seems like a nice guy and he's thirsty for Val."

"He's not thirsty." Val shrugged. "He's just being polite."

Olivia crossed her arms, glancing at Aleysha but pointing in Val's direction. "And that is why you needed this, because you can't tell when a guy is flirting with you anymore."

"It doesn't matter. I'm not available right now," Val objected. Thankfully, Philip returned, interrupting Olivia's third-degree.

"Where's Étienne?" Olivia asked.

"He'll be back. He's getting some things out of my car."

Philip stood directly beside Val. She couldn't help but breathe in his scent—something crisp, like the sea, mixed with the primitive undertone of skin and heat. The aroma wrapped itself like a dense fog around her brain, making it difficult to think.

His face lit up with a knowing smirk.

Great. He'd caught her sniffing him.

Luckily, the strains of a Maluma remix exploded over the speakers. Olivia jumped up from the chair, dragging Aleysha in her wake. This was what she'd come for. She turned to Philip. "Do you want to dance?"

Panic blazed across his face. "I don't really dance."

An unexpected wave of disappointment surged through Val, but she'd come to dance and wasn't going to sit out one of her favorite songs because it wasn't something he enjoyed. She indicated the dance floor behind her with a jab of her thumb. "I like this song, so…"

He quirked a smile at her that was equal parts impish and relieved. "I'll enjoy the show."

She gasped at his audacity. As if she'd come to be watched. "Have it your way." She turned away to join Olivia and Aleysha. She normally hated being the center of attention, but Philip's gaze was a velvet caress sliding across her skin, snaking its way into the dark corners of her body. She would never again be at another man's mercy, but that didn't mean she didn't enjoy being the focus of someone's desire. She gave herself up to the music, but also to the pleasure of his admiration, until she was nothing but sound and motion and heat.

Chapter Two

When Philip begrudgingly agreed to let Étienne bring him to a club in East Ward, of all places, he'd expected to have a few drinks while he watched his much more interesting friend captivate everyone's attention with his larger-than-life personality. He hadn't expected to meet anyone, much less make a personal connection. He'd only intended on doing his duty as Étienne's straight-man sidekick before heading home, hopefully without a headache.

Meeting Val had been an unexpected surprise. She was intelligent, funny in an unselfconscious way and able to let go, which was something he had difficulty doing.

It made her, without a doubt, one of the sexiest women he'd ever met.

If there had been any doubt on the matter, watching her dance had resolved that. She was having such a good time, it was infectious, and he very nearly joined her before he remembered how bad he was at it.

He had a feeling she was the kind of woman who could make him try anything.

She was also the kind of woman who'd probably hate him when she found out that the company slowly reshaping her community was in fact his family's company, Wagner Developments, the one he was poised to inherit.

Hers was a common enough pushback from the communities they worked in. Investors and city managers were usually happy when Wagner Developments won a project, but each community responded differently. Philip knew about groups like the East Ward Fair Housing Coalition, and his father had always resisted working with them. His father wasn't big on compromise, especially when it involved his vision for a project, and East Ward's waterfront project was their biggest one yet.

His father saw the community groups as an inconvenience. But over the years, they'd grown savvier, more organized. Philip thought it was a mistake for his father to discount the importance of these groups. He'd have to drag his father along on this one, as well.

Though his father had built the company from very little capital and sheer force of will, Philip was responsible for modernizing its style. He also strove to incorporate energy efficiencies and the smooth integration of green spaces into his city projects. His father had resisted initially, afraid of diluting the brand, until he was forced to acknowledge that it was the reason they'd become so competitive. Andreas Wagner rarely gave out compliments, so it had been a big win for Philip.

His instincts told him that someone like Val wouldn't be moved by any of that. All she'd see was his big bad corporation coming in to take away her livelihood, even toss her out of her home. She wouldn't give him the time of day if she knew who he was.

There was something about her that made this outcome difficult to accept.

He caught sight of her in mid-laugh. Her dark hair hung in thick curls down to her waist, beneath which rose the firm swell of her bottom and strong, shapely legs. Her body moved in a sinuous curve, and his mind teemed with all the ways he could bend its geography to his desires.

He gulped his beer, as if that could do anything to cool him down.

Étienne spoke to him from somewhere, and it was

with real effort that he tore his attention away from her to focus on his friend.

"We're leaving soon." Étienne's hand rested possessively on the small of Malena's back. She smiled, bedazzling Philip with the almost unnatural whiteness of her teeth. "You're okay to drive yourself home?"

"I've only had two beers."

"Such self-restraint," Malena purred.

Étienne made a face. "No, that's Philip all the time."

Philip didn't disagree with him. He couldn't even remember the last time he'd had a buzz.

When Val returned, breathless from dancing, he was seized with a sudden, stupid happiness that she'd come back to sit with him. A sheen of sweat beaded on her forehead, which she blotted away with a napkin. "That was fun," Val said between gasps.

He made to respond but a group descended on the tables near them. Between their loud voices and the music itself, there was no way to hold a conversation.

Philip leaned in to be heard by Val. "You mentioned you were leaving soon. Can I give you a ride home?"

A frown tugged at the edge of her lips and he immediately understood his mistake. She'd known him all of two hours, and here he was, asking to take her home. He searched for a way to assuage her.

"I can leave my information with your cousin. Étienne knows where to find me."

A glance at Étienne's waggling eyebrows elicited a smile from Val, and she visibly relaxed. She called Olivia away from where she was engaged in an animated conversation with Aleysha. "*Oye*, Philip wants to give you his number."

Olivia tore her eyes away from Aleysha, scanning Philip up and down. "Why? Shouldn't he be giving you his number? It's pretty clear I'm with Aleysha, right?"

"No, *tonta*," Val shouted in exasperation. "Philip is giving me a ride home, so I want you to get his number."

Olivia pulled out her phone, slid her thumb across the screen and handed it to Philip. Her features darkened, her eyes flashing with a menace she did nothing to hide. A momentary pause between songs left the club in a parenthesis of silence, making Olivia's words ring clear. "Nothing better happen to her, pretty boy. I got ways of tracking people down."

Étienne patted his wide chest. "No worries. I know where this one lives."

Olivia's frown disappeared, replaced with a comically gleaming smile. "Oh, good. Otherwise, I'd have to hack into his life and wreck him. Wouldn't want that now, would you?"

Olivia had gone from goddess to low-key assassin in zero to three seconds, which Philip found impressive—and intimidating. Before he could answer, Val interjected, "You guys can stop treating me like a three-year-old."

"They don't want anything to happen to you." Philip leaned in, admiring the sparkle of her skin under the lights. His eyes were drawn to her, no matter who in their group was speaking, and he struggled not to stare again. "They're all worried about you, but who's going to protect me from you?"

She gave him a slow smile, followed by a lazy shrug. "Looks like you're on your own." She was so close her nose nearly brushed his, and it took all his self-control not to drag it along the length of hers.

"All right, then, let's bounce," she said, sliding off her chair. He followed her as she said goodbye to at least fifty people with excruciating slowness before they finally made it out into the cool night. Philip placed a light hand on her arm to indicate the direction they should go.

Silk.

That's what her skin felt like beneath his fingers. She glanced at him with unfocused eyes, nostrils flaring with her sharp intake of breath.

"My car's over here." He gestured in the direction of his black Alfa Romeo Giulia Quadrifoglio.

Val squinted, then faced him, a flicker of surprise racing over her features. The car had been an indulgence when one of his designs had won an important commercial contract. Except now, with Val, he wondered if maybe it wasn't too much. He wanted her to like it. To like him. It was suddenly of the utmost importance to him.

She reached out to touch the metallic paint. "So pretty," she whispered.

Philip sighed. "My dream car, though Étienne never misses a chance to drive her."

"And you let him?" she answered, hugging herself against a breeze that blew in over the river. It had been an unseasonably warm April but the night air still nipped with the memory of winter.

Philip shrugged out of his jacket and draped it over her shoulders. "He's my best friend."

Val considered him for a moment before turning away. "I'd be too scared to take it out of the parking garage." She snuggled into his jacket, which distracted him a beat longer than it should have before he remembered himself and unlocked the door. She paused as she stepped inside the car. "You're not some kind of billionaire, slumming it with the common folk, are you?"

"No. And I would hardly call spending time with you 'slumming it.'"

"What would you call it, then?" Her face was so close to his—and the defiant tilt of her chin brought her even closer—it sent his thoughts swirling into chaos.

"A very good night."

She pursed her lips, but it was clear from the smile she bit back that she liked his answer. Philip wasn't actually a flirt by disposition. His father had taught him to think twice, even three times before he spoke for fear he might reveal weaknesses that others could exploit.

But with Val, he was letting all kinds of foolish things come out of his mouth, and he had to stop that or he might reveal more than he was ready to.

Once settled in the driver's seat, he switched on the heat, the warm air pushing the exquisite notes of her fragrance through the interior of the car. He inhaled, which was a huge mistake. It snaked around him, inside him, until it was all he could taste.

Of course, she was oblivious to the minor crisis her proximity caused. "Whatever you're up to, thank you." She slipped her arms into the oversize sleeves, buttoning the jacket closed. "I hadn't planned on being anywhere outside the club and didn't bring a jacket."

Her voice, which he discovered was deep and sharp when it wasn't competing with loud music, brushed up against him with the same overwhelming intensity as her fragrance. "My jacket's never looked better."

He pulled out of Aguardiente's parking lot, concentrating on Val's street directions. He was lightheaded and scattered as he merged into the trickle of traffic along the boulevard.

"How long has Étienne known Malena?"

Philip glanced at her. "A few months. Étienne is taken with her. Do you know her well?"

Val shrugged. "Well enough. Gorgeous. Smart. A real type-A personality."

"Étienne is the same way." Philip chuckled. "He's always running at top speed, and he hasn't yet met anyone who can slow him down."

"I guess that makes them either terrible or perfect for each other." Out of the corner of his eye, he caught sight of her lips kicking up into a smile before she turned to look out the window. Philip loved driving, but at that moment, he wished he didn't have to. He wanted to stare at her profile as the lights flashed by, watch them trip themselves in her hair and stream around her nose and cheeks. The disparate parts of her face were nothing extraordinary by themselves, but arranged as they were, they captivated him.

"How about you?" she asked. "Have you ever met someone who made you want to slow down?"

He tore himself away from the prosaic meditation on her cheekbones. "Maybe." He gave her a sidelong glance. "I'm not sure yet."

Val's husky laugh complicated his predicament tenfold. "You are one smooth guy, Philip. You managed to flatter me and avoid the question at the same time."

"Touché." Philip grinned. "I dated someone while studying for my MBA. We were together for three years, and I thought we might be able to make things more permanent between us. But then her career exploded and there just wasn't any room left for me."

"Ouch."

"Ouch, indeed."

"What was her career anyway?"

"Choreographer."

"Ah," Val said. "Hence the look of terror when I asked you to dance."

"Maybe." He couldn't blame his ex for his inability to dance. He'd hated dancing long before he'd met her. "Your turn."

Val exhaled noisily, the exasperation clear. "That's the problem with living in the same neighborhood all your life. Everybody knows everybody else's business." She squirmed in her seat, her legs dangerously distracting to his driving. "My ex and I dated for over two years until last summer, when I found out, very much in public, that he was committed to someone else."

"In Aguardiente?"

"Bingo."

"Ouch."

"Ouch, indeed," she mimicked, at which they both laughed.

"You know, that's the first time I've actually laughed about breaking up with Luke."

They were at a traffic light, waiting for it to turn green. Philip held her gaze—he couldn't look away if he wanted. "Still stings, doesn't it?"

"Yeah, especially when everyone keeps reminding you how bad it was, or how sorry they are that it happened. Isn't it the same for you?"

"I'd say a little less now."

"Huh." She turned away to stare out the window again, a more troubled expression reflected back against the backdrop of lights illuminating the darkness. It was clear that the relationship had brought her pain, and she'd endured it in a public way. She'd probably provided endless grist for the local rumor mill. This insight triggered something fierce and protective within him.

A horn honked behind him, and he drew his eyes away from her to focus on the road. After a few quiet minutes, they were on Clemente Avenue, a name Philip recalled, not only from their earlier conversation, but also from his work on the East Ward project. It was surreal to see this area outside of the context of his company's business plans, its sleeping buildings almost vulnerable at this dark hour.

He pulled into an empty spot in front of a darkened storefront. The street was quiet, the neighborhood nothing like the one he lived in, characterized by starchy doormen and expensive security cameras. A niggling of guilt at the back of his mind reminded him of their earlier conversation about Wagner Developments, while street signs with familiar names mocked him. The light-rail station and old factory that were central to the company's plans were two blocks away, and the sprawling tenement they'd purchased for renovation, the Victoria, was on this same street. Each landmark loomed ominous and bleak over them. Val wouldn't take a second step with him if she knew of his company's interests in this area.

"Here I am." She pointed at a dark building on the corner, illuminated only by a flickering streetlamp.

He maneuvered into a parking space beneath the

streetlamp and shut off the ignition. Before Val could get her door open, he made sure to be there, offering his hand for support. Under the glow of the lamp, he noticed the calluses punctuating the smooth skin of her palm, while thin scars decorated her hand like intricate latticework threaded through otherwise flawless skin. He could easily spend hours studying the topography of her fingers.

"You live here?" he asked, squinting to make out the red, white and blue awning sign that read Navarro's Family Restaurant. Yes, this address was far too familiar and the sinking feeling grew more acute.

"Upstairs," she answered.

"A mixed-use." He recited the other details to himself. Four story. Eight units. Ground floor commercial space. Storage basement. He might as well have been reading directly from his design specs.

"All in one place." Her voice pulled him out of his head. "My parents established the restaurant when they moved from Puerto Rico and thought it would be efficient to rent the floor directly above it." She glanced up at him, her brown eyes nearly black in the dim light. "It means everything to me. To us," she murmured, almost to herself.

A curl clinging to her cheek beckoned to be smoothed behind her ear. He fisted his hand instead, repressing the impulse. "My father feels that way about his business. It's like another child to him." He didn't add that his father loved his business almost to the exclusion of everyone else.

"It really is like having a baby." She held on to

him as she steadied herself on the pavement. "I…I know it's late, but would you like some coffee before you go?"

He should go home. He, of all people, shouldn't be with this person here, of all places.

"I'd love some."

She led him around the side of the building to unlock a door at the top of a short flight of stone stairs. An automatic light flared to life from a fluorescent bulb above, forcing Philip to blink away the brightness. He was accustomed to assessing the character of buildings, and this one possessed it in spades. The walls were painted a flawless ecru and gold, and framed prints and pictures decorated the surface at perfectly spaced out intervals. Nothing like the antiseptic modernity of the foyer in his apartment building, where everything gleamed with premeditated elegance.

"Whoever maintains this building does a good job of keeping it up," he said.

"All the tenants pitch in to take care of it." She paused in front of a metal box next to another door and flipped the lid to punch in a code on the keypad.

Alarm deactivated, they stepped inside. Val switched on more lights and led him through an immaculate kitchen. They emerged behind a refrigerated service counter where pastries and sweets were arranged in tempting display. Woven baskets lined the back walls, while cake holders full of unfamiliar, cellophane-wrapped treats rested on the shelves.

Philip didn't know what he'd expected from the unassuming exterior, but this cozy space was not it. Accustomed to the more calculated elegance of the restaurants he usually frequented, he was unprepared for the warmth that was so much like the woman who now kicked off her heels to slip into a pair of purple Crocs.

"You're short," he laughed, placing a hand on the top of her head. She barely grazed his chin.

"That's why I wear these torture devices." She quirked an eyebrow at him as she took his hand from her head and held it. The heat of her skin pressed warm and urgent into his. "Do you mind?"

"There's nothing about you that I mind, so far."

"Give it time." She shrugged his jacket off her shoulders and handed it to him. He slung it over his arm, thinking it best to spare her the sight of him burying his nose in the fragrance she'd left behind.

"I'll go in the back and make you a cup of coffee. Do you want regular, or something a little stronger, like espresso?"

"Espresso sounds good."

"Won't it keep you up?"

"No, it generally has the opposite effect on me. Weird biology, I suppose."

Her expression uncertain, she disappeared behind the counter. The sound of opening cabinets and clanging pots cut through the silence. Philip browsed the family pictures of different children lining the walls, including an adorable young girl that had to be Val. A narrow glass case held basketball, base-ball and cheerleading trophies. He circled the case, searching for the ones with Val's name and found several track-and-field statuettes. He recalled her strong legs as she danced and pushed that distract-ing image out of his mind. A Puerto Rican flag hung from the ceiling alongside an American one, it's broad, alternating red-and-white stripes and blue triangle imprinted with a single white star.

Accent walls not hung with photos were covered in murals depicting tropical scenes. One stood out, the images more stylized than the others. He stood before a land of coconut trees, white sand and peril-ous rocks plunging into the sea. Dense forests abutted the base of mountains that scraped against the bluest blue of the sky. There was no doubt. The painter was a gifted artist, delivering on the promise of an island tableau in the middle of a concrete jungle.

Coffee burbled from the kitchen, pulling him away from his thoughts. He followed the sound and aroma, struck by the odd jolt of happiness at the sight of Val, the way he'd felt when she'd returned from her dance. He found her standing in front of the stove, tending to an angular metal coffee machine.

"What's that?" he asked, as a thin stream of black liquid escaped the seam and slid down, hissing into the flames.

"A *cafetera*." She slipped on a worn cooking mitt and poured out the coffee.

"Coffee maker," he murmured.

Val nodded. "A Moka machine, essentially. Do you speak Spanish?"

"Just enough to get into trouble."

Val nodded thoughtfully. "Damn. Now I won't be able to gossip about you."

"Sorry to disappoint."

"Told you I'd do something you'd mind. Milk and sugar?"

"No milk, no sugar. I prefer my coffee bitter."

Val poured a small cup with a flair that brought a smile to his face. He took a sip, relishing the deep, nutty flavor. "This is good. Thank you."

She gave a small bow before pulling two stools from against the wall and inviting him to sit next to her. The hum of the refrigerator and the clicking of the icebox punctuated the silence as he sipped, savoring the heat and comfort of the brew.

"It must be a lot of pressure," Val said at length.

Philip blinked in confusion. "What's a lot of pressure?"

She shrugged. "Working for the company that your father owns."

The thread of their earlier conversation returned to him. "It is but I was lucky, I guess. I happened to land in a career I enjoy. I don't know what things might have been like if I'd hated my work. Isn't it the same for you? Don't you work with your father, too?"

Val nodded. "We're co-owners. I'm the oldest, so things have always fallen on my shoulders. But I lucked out, too. I love cooking and I can't imagine myself doing anything else." Val stood, surprising him with her sudden explosion of motion. "I have an idea." She raced around the kitchen, collecting a whirlwind of ingredients.

Philip drained the last of his small cup. "What are you up to now?" He watched as she broke chunks of dark chocolate into the pan, whisking it as it melted.

"It's a surprise." She gave him a bone-melting smile before returning to her work. She added cream and a pinch of powder that smelled like nutmeg, stirring the dark brown liquid. She removed the pan from the fire, set it aside and opened the double-door refrigerator, rummaging inside until she brought out a cake dish. Philip leaned on his hand and watched; her fluid movements were full of the confidence of knowing a space intimately.

"If you're the oldest, how many brothers and sisters do you have?" he asked.

Val looked up from her work. "One each." She poked the air with the silver cake cutter as she spoke. "There's Natalía but we call her Nati. And Rafael is Rafi."

"And what's Val short for?"

She leaned in close as if she were sharing a secret. "Valeria."

"Pretty. Like you."

Val glanced down to cut the cake but she could not hide her smile completely. "You're a flirt."

"Not usually." The desire that had so befuddled him in the car morphed into something warm and soft, like a homemade quilt his mother had once made in one of her domestic arts phases. The stitching had grown soft with overuse and the edges of the squares faded but he had spent many nights wrapped inside of it, soothed as if by her own hand.

"Anyway, this kitchen is my empire," she continued, though there was a breathless quality to her words. "Rafi teaches math at the high school and Nati has one year left to finish her medical degree. I'm already planning her graduation party. I was thinking of doing it at Aguardiente, since there's both a kitchen and a dance area." She pulled two plates from the cupboard. "Wow, I'm taking up all the oxygen in the room."

"You're lovely when you talk."

Val dipped her head again, a smile hidden behind a curtain of thick, curly hair. This was a new side of her and he liked it. Shy Val, the one who didn't know what to do with a compliment.

"How about you?" she asked.

"Me? No, I'm an only child, with all that implies."

She wrinkled her nose. "Ugh, I bet you're so spoiled."

"The worst."

She chortled as she picked up two plates and filled them with slices of a very wet cake before setting them in front of him. She returned with the pot of melted chocolate and poured the now-cooled liquid into a cup, handing it to him. Val fussing over him made him feel positively giddy. He raised the cup and took a sip. Chocolate and nutmeg melted on his tongue, sending a surge of pleasure through him.

"Puerto Rican hot chocolate," she said, taking her seat again. "Maybe the sugar will perk you up."

"You're worried about me falling asleep at the wheel." The thought of her fretting over his well-being gave him a warm feeling inside.

"Can't help that you have strange biology. This is how *I'm* made. I'm a worrier."

His eyes flickered to her strong hands, admiring the signs of use, and he wondered what other things she created with them. "No one's worried about me in a very long time."

He was learning to read her, so he was ready for her zinger. "In my family, worrying is an Olympic sport, so if you ever need someone to worry about you, feel free to borrow any of us."

He smiled into his cup. "I appreciate the offer."

If the chocolate had been bliss, the cake was pure decadence. Drenched in a thick vanilla cream, it slid smooth and potent over his tongue, its sweetness just shy of unbearable. "This tres leches is wrecking me."

Her proud smile nearly provoked a desire to cast the cake aside and kiss her. "It's my Saturday Special. I offer it together with flan and crème brûlée. Do you want to try them, also?" She made to step away, but he caught her by the hand before she could pull some other wonderful delight from what he was starting to think was a magical refrigerator.

"No, it's too much. Save it for next time." He paused, steeling himself. "That is, if next time is okay with you."

She settled onto the stool, shuffling her feet into

and out of her Crocs. "I wasn't really looking for anything tonight."

"Neither was I. But here we are."

Her eyes flicked away again. "That breakup I told you about? That was the last time I've been with anyone."

"Same. It's been a while for me, too." Maybe too long, if his complete lack of confidence right now was any indication.

"Just managing expectations." She poked at her cake, swirling the fork in the fragrant cream. "I'm really not up for anything serious."

"That's fair."

She took a bite, chewing slowly, the gears of her mind visibly working. He didn't rush her, and his patience was rewarded when, after a full minute, she said, "Okay. Next Saturday. I don't work Sundays."

Joy surged at her words, but the exultation was short-lived. Who he was and what his company was doing in East Ward hung like a shadow in the darkest part of his brain, prodding him in accusation. And still, the confession died in his throat.

The gleam of passing headlights sneaked in under the shutters of the front windows, leaving the blush of sunrise after the car lights had passed.

"I can't believe what time it is," Val said as they carried the plates to the sink.

"I've got these," Philip said, taking the sponge and soap from her.

Val crossed her arms, watching him work. "You know, I already said yes."

Philip raised an eyebrow at her. "That's not why I'm doing it. It's only fair that if you cook, I clean up."

"Hmm," she purred, and it was obvious she was having a quiet laugh at his expense. Another version of her to file away.

The lack of sleep or the sugar rush made him reckless, because he was talking without even the pretext of thinking about what he was saying. "What if I can't wait until next Saturday?"

Val spread her arms to indicate the kitchen. "My culinary empire demands my complete attention during the week."

Philip set down the last plate and shut off the water. "But I know where you live."

"It's like that?" she whispered.

"It's like that," he answered, and she was suddenly so close, if he leaned forward, it would be impossibly easy to kiss her. And he wanted to kiss her badly; the wanting burned hot in his chest. But he couldn't. It would be a lie. He couldn't kiss her if he wasn't able to be fully himself.

He pulled back and took out his phone instead. "Can I have your number?"

Val blinked several times, dispelling what lingered of the moment before reciting the number to him. Her phone dinged somewhere with his text. Sensible, yet this pedestrian exchange felt momentous to him. She was in his contacts now. Something of hers that he could return to.

He gathered his things and she accompanied him

to the main exit. He stepped out under a lightening sky, which contrasted with the partially dim streetlamp that flickered sporadically, mocking his lack of courage. *Just tell her*, it seemed to say.

He'd ruin everything if he did. And he wanted to do this again. Wanted her to like him for him and not judge him by what he did, which she would inevitably do if she knew. And given the little he'd learned about her, she would judge him hard.

He pressed the button on the fob to unlock his car door, glancing back at the sight of her leaning against the doorjamb with arms crossed, her purple Crocs at odds with the black-and-silver outfit. Jarring, yet so domestic. It was charming.

"We broke night!" she called out, pointing at the brightening sky, her voice ricocheting across the empty avenue.

He looked up at the gathering morning, a different person than he'd been the day before. It took extraordinary effort not to close the space separating them and give in to the indulgence her lips promised— sweet and intoxicating like the chocolate and cake she'd served him. But he knew if he did, it wouldn't taste sweet at all, but bitter, like guilt seasoned with a dash of cowardice.

He waved goodbye instead, before climbing into his car and pulling away.

Chapter Three

After Philip left, Val sneaked quietly upstairs to the half apartment she shared with her sister, the other half occupied by Rafi and their father. When their mother was still alive, they combined both sections to create one unit, separated only by a door. But as soon as Val began culinary arts school, her father separated them again, allowing the girls to have one side while he stayed with Rafi on the other, giving everyone a measure of privacy without sending any of the Navarro children into the world to look for it.

She slipped into her bedroom, shutting the door softly so the reverberations wouldn't wake her sister, who was sleeping like a normal person should on a Saturday morning.

Val wasn't looking for a relationship, had even told Olivia she wasn't interested. She had bigger problems to worry about—keeping developers from devouring her neighborhood, running the restaurant and taking care of her family. Nati had one more year of med school left to go, and Rafi, bless him, spent all his money on his classroom.

But Philip was…incredibly tempting.

Val had no business feeling this way. She'd been through all this before. Getting wildly infatuated as if it were the solution to all her problems. She wasn't going to do that again. She had to come down from the high of spending half the night with a person that didn't include sex. There had been nothing to distract her from him.

And damn if it hadn't been amazing.

Besides Philip's good looks, she liked his little gestures in a way that surprised her. Holding doors open, offering her his jacket, steadying her when she stumbled. The man was obviously well-off, but that didn't prevent him from getting his hands dirty and washing dishes. As if it was the most normal thing in the world to get up and wash a strange woman's plates.

They even liked the same things, and he didn't mind geeking out with her.

Val peeled off her outfit and hung it on a chair to be dry-cleaned, debating whether to return it to Olivia or not. It would always be the outfit in which she first met Philip, with its too-low décolletage and too-short bottom imprinted with echoes of this night.

But that made no sense. She'd only just met him. There was no reason to make a monument out of it.

She took the fastest shower in history and pulled on her favorite pajamas—soft cotton Yoda print pants and matching green shirt with the phrase Stay for Some Soup, You Must—a gag gift from Nati.

Val tucked herself in, shoving thoughts of Philip firmly away. Not this time. Even if their attraction had been immediate, Val wasn't going to walk that road again. Luke had taken a lot from her, but the worst thing he'd stolen was her ability to trust.

And worse, he'd humiliated her in front of everybody. Her friends and her cousin had come to her defense, but it had only compounded the betrayal with the one thing she couldn't tolerate from anyone.

Pity.

Val wasn't one to be pitied.

So for months, she'd stuck to her restaurant. Her family. Tried to give her heart the space to heal.

It had been hard work and she wasn't about to undo it for a new pretty face and a fancy car. Even Philip's attitude toward East Ward's development was a little suspect. Nope. She wouldn't play the fool again for anyone. No matter how sexy he looked or how good he smelled…

She picked up the *Star Wars* novel she'd been reading, but after a few paragraphs, exhaustion overtook her. In her increasingly dissociative state, images of Philip fused with whatever lay scattered in the clapboard box of her unconscious until she drifted into a dream.

She stood by the sea, a place she'd visited with her family as a child. The glimmer of a half-hidden sun rose over the horizon, as a man moved toward her. A bronze-tinged heat suffused her, coming in equal measures from both the sun and the man who approached. Val was torn between the impulse to wait for him or to run away and hide in the caves embedded in the rock cliff. Frozen in place, the dream dissipated before she could do either.

When Val woke, she looked at the clock and calculated that she had exactly eighteen minutes to get down to the restaurant for the lunch rush.

She was out of bed and dressed in record time even though her body was screaming for more sleep. Thank God she'd prepped the food yesterday afternoon before heading to the salon to get her nails done. That way, her father wouldn't have as much to do in the morning.

She checked her phone, nudging away the disappointment when she found no new messages, and stuffed it in the back pocket of her jeans. Racing downstairs, she burst through the back door of the restaurant, the aroma of coffee freezing her in her tracks, reminding her that she hadn't had anything for breakfast.

"I'm losing my mind," she muttered as she reached

beneath the breakfast counter for a mug. "How did I leave my house without coffee?"

"Maybe you have something on your mind." Nati handed her a mug of coffee exactly the way Val liked it—steeped with cream and sugar. But Nati didn't fool her. She smiled so widely, she looked cartoonish.

"What's got into you?" Val grumbled as she took a long, hearty sip of her loaded *café con leche*.

Nati's tightly coiled, dark blond curls bobbed as she tried to suppress a girlish giggle, though the ruthless gleam of her green eyes was anything but innocent. She had taken after their mother's side of the family, with her lighter hair and complexion, whereas Val and Rafi were dark in every way, just like their father. "Hmm, nothing. I just heard from a little birdie that you had fun last night, that's all." Nati crossed her arms, oblivious to Angela trying to squeeze by her with a tray of roasted pork.

"A harpy's more like it," Val snapped. "*Dios mío*, the day's barely started—"

"It's already eleven o'clock—"

"And Olivia's already gossiping? I'm surrounded by predators."

Nati's body vibrated with barely suppressed laughter. "So, tell me about him."

"I think they need *plátanos* out front." Val plucked a slice of plum cake from an overfilled cake dish and slipped into the kitchen, hoping her sister might take the hint and go away.

She had no such luck. "Don't try to boss me around. Spill."

Val used her fingertips to collect the crumbs that fell on the kitchen counter. "I met a guy. We hung out. That's. All."

"That's all? You stayed out all night and all you did was hang out?"

"It wasn't all night. And you can hang out with a man without having sex."

"There's also no shame in a woman taking a man home if that's what she wants," Nati retorted. A snarky response sat on the tip of Val's tongue when her phone vibrated. Her irritation evaporated when she read the notification with Philip's name.

"*Esa sonrisa!* Who's making you smile like that?"

Val looked up, glowering at her sister. *"¡Ay, cal-late!"*

"Don't tell me to shut up," Nati retorted between giggles.

"Then go away." Younger siblings were supposed to grow out of being annoying, but Nati had missed that developmental milestone.

Val settled in to read Philip's text message.

Hey. What are you up to?

Trying not to murder my sister, she quickly typed.

When he responded with several laugh emojis, Val imagined the husky, resonant quality of his voice, the way his laugh bubbled up, warm and masculine, through his body. She remembered the way the sound had coiled around her like a silk scarf, how it had sent electric pulses racing down her spine. Her father called Val but Nati answered instead.

"I'm coming, Papi," Nati shouted. "Val needs to be alone with her phone."

Val rolled her eyes before returning to her phone. She had another text.

What's the daily special?

Val was proud of her stewed and grilled dishes, introducing unconventional ingredients to traditional recipes with mostly successful results. She was tempted to invite him over, then thought better of it. Not only was it contrary to her commitment to keeping things cool between them, but her entire family was working the restaurant today, and she'd rather shove a sea star under her toenail than subject anyone to that baptism by fire.

She texted an answer, which started off a brisk exchange.

Braised codfish with eggplant over a bed of cassava, avocado and grilled onions

Sounds delicious

And roasted goat with rosemary potatoes

Maybe not

You haven't lived until you've had my father's goat

I'll take your word for it

Bet I can talk you into trying it

Bet you can talk me into anything

His words sent splinters of fire like shrapnel throughout her body. She tingled, her skin stretched too thin, too tight to inhabit, and her body called for a kind of relief she knew she wouldn't soon find.

She typed and retyped her message, her fumbling fingers missing the intended letters until the words made sense. The last thing the lunch rush needed was for her to lose her head.

I've got to run. Can I text you later?

Anytime. And thank you for last night. It was…

Val waited, counting the seconds, growing impatient when ten had gone by without any follow-up.

It was…?

A beat and then… It was incomparable.
Val smiled, then giggled, biting her lip to stifle

the ridiculous sound. She breathed loudly through her nose, exhaling as if she'd just run a marathon before typing:

That's a big word.

The laugh emoji came instantaneously.

I have a big...vocabulary

Val groaned aloud.

So lame.

They texted their goodbyes, after which Val stood for a moment longer in the kitchen, trying to steady her racing heart. *Calmate*, she scolded, willing herself to come back down to earth. It was just a few text messages, that's all. No need to act like a punch-drunk teenager. It's not like he'd done anything special to make her feel all queasy inside.

Val sought out her father—the only person who could ground her in reality. Work was the perfect antidote to the way her body had responded to Philip's attention.

She found him at his usual post, working the cash register. His dark curls hung over his forehead, his deep brown eyes clear and friendly as he murmured something to the young woman he was serving, resulting in shared laughter. He wore a pale yellow guayabera under his apron. The pockets of the short-sleeved, button-down shirt bulged with pens, paper clips, bits of paper and rubber bands, a habit Rafi had inherited, as well. Whoever helped Papi with his laundry had to make sure to check all the pockets or there was no way of knowing what they'd find in the dryer.

"Papi, where do you want me?"

"Mijita." He smiled as if twenty customers weren't in line, waiting to be served. Whenever he saw Val, or any of his children, his face lit up as if he'd won the Powerball.

"Take the à la carte line. Angela isn't having a good day. Send Nati out to serve."

"Pobrecita," Val said as she took a post next to Angela, who'd recently lost her husband and often went into the office to pray for comfort to a wall calendar of Father Pius next to a picture of Val's late mother. Val always made a point to be extra patient with Angela. After all, the Navarros were well acquainted with the ebb and flow of grief.

Val jumped into the workflow, hoping to put Philip out of her mind. She grabbed plates for dining in, and carryout containers for to-go customers. She breathed in the homemade *sazón* she used to season the rice, which always left her fingertips orange. The sting of tomato sauce and cilantro in her stewed chicken battled with the sharp bite of onion in her *bistéc encebollado*. She was in constant motion, retreating to the kitchen to refill hot plates or fulfill a custom order.

Sometimes she redirected customers to the sandwich and bakery line, where Rafi sold bread and baked goods, filling wax bags with *alcapúrrias*, *empanadas*, *papas rellenas*, *surullitos* and other Caribbean snack foods. Val concentrated extra hard to keep her thoughts from wandering to Philip.

As usual, the place was packed and loud, with the speakers pumping old-school salsa and merengue. Almost everyone knew each other, but the clientele was changing. Families that had been in the neighborhood had begun to move out, replaced by a revolving door of new people Val didn't recognize. She followed her father's example and was respectful to everyone who frequented their restaurant, but it was hard to watch people she'd known all her life struggle and disappear because a group of suits somewhere had decided East Ward was a good place to make money.

By late afternoon, the rush had dwindled, except for a pair of older women who were having coffee and dessert after spending most of the day shopping. The front doorbell chimed as it opened and a familiar voice cut across the low drone of their conversation.

"Darth Cupcake!"

"Here we go," Val muttered.

"How's my girl? Nati, has your sister recovered from last night?" Olivia began, and Val couldn't help but groan inwardly.

"Take a breath, will you? I can't believe you already put my business out there."

Nati grinned maniacally, and Val realized she'd have to fight off not one, but two harpies. "I bet she was with that guy she was texting before."

"Traitor," Val scolded. "I'm not talking about Philip with you two."

"Philip?" Rafi asked as he wandered over, wiping his hands on his apron. He was the spitting image of his father, except for a sharpening of his cheekbones and jaw, which was entirely their mother. "Who's Philip?"

"A guy your sister spent the night with," Olivia answered.

"What the hell, Olivia!" Val retorted. Nati and Olivia cackled while Rafi straightened to attention, his eyes wide with surprise.

"Did you get your freak on, big sis?" he asked, his tone more serious than his words implied.

"No! I did not get my freak on. We hung out. I mean, I just met him last night."

Rafi put his arm around Val's shoulder, squeezing her to him. "You don't have to be ashamed of a little hit-and-run every now and then."

Val threw her hands up in the air. "This conversation cannot be happening."

"No pierdas la cabeza, bonita." Nati sang her usual admonishment for Val not to lose her head. "We like to tease you because you give such good game. So, are you going to see him again?"

The three of them stared at her bug-eyed, as if they were waiting for the next scene in a telenovela. Val deflated. She couldn't fight them, any more than she could stop the sun from setting. "We're going out next Saturday."

"Not gonna lie," Olivia said. "He's good-looking, in that all-American, Wonder Bread sort of way, you know? The total opposite of brooding Luke."

"Why do you guys always bring up Luke?" Val huffed. To her relief, Papi appeared, arms crossed, giving the group a stern look.

"*Qué pasó aquí?* Are we holding a family meeting instead of working?"

"Nothing, Papi." Val threw them all a look of pure venom, heading off anything Olivia or Nati might say to embarrass her.

"Good, because those customers aren't going to serve themselves."

"Yes, sir," Nati said, tugging Rafi behind her. Olivia gave Val a smirk that promised more teasing before she picked up a free newspaper from the rack and took a seat at the lunch counter.

Her father put an arm around Val's shoulders, and she melted into his hug. He was as tall as she was, his face lined but handsome. He'd worked hard all his life, first in his family's plantation fields on the island, then at the restaurant, and had a slender but strong body to show for it.

"So, this guy you went out with. Does he have any money?"

"Don't tell me you were eavesdropping."

Her horror softened when he tweaked her nose. "Just kidding. I'm not too old to joke around."

"Obviously not." She scowled when he released her.

"As long as he's not like that other guy, I don't care how much money he has," he said with uncharacteristic vehemence. Val and her father worked side by side in Navarro's most days, but it was only then that she understood what her brokenhearted condition of the last several months must have seemed like to him.

They went to their separate workstations, Val only too happy to end that discussion. She wasn't ready to put Philip in the same headspace as Luke. In fact, thoughts of Luke were best left out of her head altogether.

By the time the restaurant closed and the family prepared for their own dinner, Val was sure she would never regain feeling in her thighs again.

"Too much dancing?" Nati teased as she set a table for them in the closed dining room.

Val rubbed the muscles of her hips. "I'm out of practice."

"I got a bachata workout routine that I do at least three times a week." Rafi set the seafood ceviche in the middle of the table and plopped down on the chair. "You should try it."

"You would think with all the running she does,

her legs would be stronger." Papi prepared each plate, serving them before setting one for himself. Val relished the aroma of lemon, cilantro and seafood that greeted her.

Rafi waved a finger in the air. "Not the same muscles. You've got to develop those again, sis."

Why did every aspect of Val's existence require a committee discussion? "I'll work on that. Thanks."

"Felicia wants to hold the community meeting at the restaurant after closing on Friday, and Papi said it was okay," Nati interjected. Felicia Morales, real estate lawyer for the East Ward Fair Housing Coalition, had built a career advising community groups advocating for responsible development.

"Has she sent out the notice of the change to everyone?" Rafi said between bites. "I haven't checked my email today."

"*Si*. Just this morning," Papi said, wiping his mouth with a paper napkin. "She's bringing in lawyers to offer pro bono consultations to the renters at the Victoria."

Val tapped the table thoughtfully. "The rent hikes and evictions are disgusting, aren't they?"

"It's like when they put that expensive gym right next to the light-rail stop that no one in the neighborhood could afford, including me." Rafi said.

Nati set a cup next to Rafi's plate. "Your salary is bank compared to what most people make here. If you can't afford it, I don't imagine anybody else around here can."

Papi served everyone another scoop of the ceviche over Rafi's protests.

"Ay, por favor. Eat. You're never gonna catch a boyfriend if you look like a skeleton," Papi teased.

Rafi took the spoon away from him and placed it in the dish. "I haven't heard any complaints so far, Papi."

Papi pulled a face, which on him was extra adorable. *"Malcriado."*

"Yeah, don't be a brat." Val took a long draft of water. After all this time, she should be immune to their banter. "Wagner Developments won't be happy until they've taken over every building, every retail space and turned East Ward into a little hipster paradise. And where does that leave us?"

"Navarro's will still be here," Nati said.

"Yeah, but for how long? Navarro's might not be shiny or chic enough for these new people. Seems all they really want is some funky veggie smoothie or something."

"I don't know." Rafi picked up a colorful paper plate from the counter in the tiny kitchen and put it on his head. "We could push the whole multicultural angle."

"That's not a half-bad idea." Nati folded the plate until it looked like a shipwrecked fishing boat and put it back on Rafi's head. He posed, batting his long, dark lashes prettily at everyone.

"No sean necios," Papi admonished, warning them not to be foolish. "We are not a cheap franchise. This is a family restaurant." Nati and Rafi

grew quiet at Papi's change of tone. "Gabriela and I, God rest her soul, we made sacrifices so that you three could have a good life. We're here to stay, and no company is going to tell us when to go."

Nati nodded, her eyes losing focus while Rafi's fork paused in midair. "Ay, Mami." He shook his head, his handsome face marred with a frown.

Val patted both their hands. Sometimes, she forgot that she wasn't the only one who'd lost a mother, or that her father had also lost a wife.

They finished their meal in silence. When Val was done, she rubbed her stomach in satisfaction. "That wasn't half-bad, even without the pepper."

"I tried to tell you," Nati said. "But your head is as hard as concrete."

"Concrete doesn't have a chance against that rock on her shoulders." Rafi scooped a forkful from the pile of seafood his father had sneakily dumped onto his plate, missing the look of satisfaction Papi gave him.

Stifling a yawn, Papi rose, giving them each a kiss on the cheek. "*Bueno*, I'm going up to bed."

"We got cleanup covered." Val's phone vibrated in her pocket. She pulled it out, and felt an automatic smile creasing her face.

"Gee, wonder who that is?" Nati teased, flicking the end of the towel against Val's hip before carrying the dishes into the kitchen.

Rafi also stood with his now-empty plate. "You guys have known each other for what, five seconds, and look at you."

"Zip it, both of you," Val snapped.

Just finished dinner, she texted Philip.

I like when you talk about food. What did you have?

Ceviche. Do you know it?

Seafood salad? Sure, I know it. What was in it?

Crab, shrimp, onions, avocado and my special seasoning.

I think I might need this recipe.

Val chuckled, looking up to see both Nati and Rafi shaking their heads before leaving her alone in the dining room so she could continue her text exchange uninterrupted.

Sorry. Secret recipe. Can't give away my trade secrets.

Are you teasing me?

It's a distinct possibility.

Val snorted. She cracked herself up sometimes.

What's your opinion on French cuisine?

The French seem to dig it.

He sent a message with several laughing emojis. She blushed, as if he'd only just invented them for her.

So Saturday. I pick you up and we go to a French place I know. Since you said you like experimenting.

Val closed her eyes. Her dream date was anyone other than herself doing the cooking.

I'd like that.

I'll send over all the details. And you should reconsider sharing your recipe.

She could just make it for him, but that would be another date and she'd barely cleared their first one.

I'm going to look into getting some sleep soon. Someone kept me up all night.

Not sorry.

Val put her phone down, her breath shaky. Nati and Rafi's banter floated over the sound of them loading the dishwasher. Philip had messaged her twice in one day, but she didn't want to read too much into it. It was one night featuring hot chocolate and cake of all things. That was it. Nothing to see here.

She'd learned the hard way that getting too close

to people too soon meant you risked being swept far away from yourself if you weren't careful. The last time she'd done that, it had cost her two years of her life and another year putting it back together again. She wasn't interested in repeating that mistake again.

Chapter Four

Philip leaned over the three-dimensional model of East Ward, comparing the Lilliputian-sized buildings with his design specs, and found them satisfactory. He had prepared himself for the questions that would soon come his way from the investor group his father was meeting with. But his mind circled around Val and their night together, settling haphazardly on a series of splintered images. Her strong hand as it cradled her coffee cup. Her eyes, which glittered whenever she was preparing to say something funny. The coconut and fruit perfume that had coiled like a steel cable around him.

He rested his finger over the model that represented her building. An average mixed-use sitting on the corner of Clemente Avenue and Muñoz Marin Boulevard. One building in an entire street full of inventory slowly being snapped up, ready to be converted into high-end housing to complement the waterfront project. It would keep Wagner Developments busy for years. And it had been Philip's design that had carried the day.

Voices floated down the hallway outside the conference room. He straightened as he always did when his father was near.

"We've been awarded a contract by the city to develop the old pencil factory complex, and the lower East Ward residential opportunity zone," his father narrated to a group of people in business dress who trailed behind him. Nodding to acknowledge Philip's presence, his father continued, "Luxury condominiums, commercial space with a unified aesthetic." He stopped before the model and swept his hand across the top, revealing his platinum and gold cuff links. "Let me introduce you to my son, Philip, the man responsible for the winning design."

Philip basked in the familiar flush of pride that came with his father's praise. He shook hands with the businesspeople, assessing each one as he did so before leading them into the conference room and making his presentation. He was the youngest in the group—he usually was. But at thirty-two years old, he had already established a reputation independent of his father's, despite being heir apparent to the corporation. He had earned his position as EVP of Project Design not because he was Andreas Wagner's son, but despite it. Unlike other sons of corporate giants, who enjoyed the fruits of their family's businesses without exerting themselves on their own merits, he'd earned everything he'd ever achieved in his career, precisely because his father believed in a ruthless meritocracy that applied even to his only son.

After the Q and A, Andreas pulled Philip aside, leaving the group to admire the scale model. "After this wraps up, several of our investors will be joining us for dinner."

Philip winced. "I have other plans."

Andreas's face darkened into a frown. He was tall—Philip had inherited his height from him. His thick gray hair complemented light, almost colorless blue eyes that contained the shadows of the forbidding Carpathian Mountains from which his family originated. "Let me guess. Étienne. How is your friend's little activity going?"

And there went the pleasure of earning his father's praise. "Little activity? You mean his award-winning photography, which is featured in every major art and fashion magazine in the world? That little activity?" Philip made the extraordinary effort to rein in the irritation toward his father that seemed to know no bounds lately. He used to admire the single-minded determination that made his father such a formidable businessman. Hell, Philip had thrown himself wholeheartedly into the family business in the hopes he could measure up to him.

But that relentlessness didn't come naturally to him. He needed more, but he wasn't sure what that more really was.

"Award-winning? Good, but are they paying him? He can't live on awards alone."

"He does well for himself."

His father glared at him, the conversation an echo of so many they'd had in their lives. His father's constant reminder that what mattered was completing the best project, making the most money and squashing anyone who got in the way. Philip had grown increasingly exhausted with hearing his father put down people just because he couldn't see the economic value in the work they did. "Still, our investors would probably like to hear more about the project from the designer himself. You can go out with Étienne anytime."

"I presented. I answered questions. Sales have never been my area of expertise. You told me so yourself."

"Parents don't like being reminded of every little criticism they make of their children."

"Please extend my deepest apologies to everyone for being unable to attend this evening."

Andreas opened his mouth but quickly closed it, rearranging his features to project the signature impassivity that marked his negotiation style.

"Philip won't be joining us," his father said, addressing the group. "He's attending a charitable function, but he has a few minutes, if you'd like to ask him anything else." Philip scowled at the easy lie, but let it stand, pushing down the flicker of anxiety that accompanied his refusal to bow to his father's wishes, a Pavlovian response he only barely curtailed.

Philip's phone vibrated, providing a welcome opportunity to break away. He excused himself to go to his office, closing the door behind him. When he answered, he couldn't help but smile at Étienne's gruff voice barreling through the telephone.

"Why are you still at work?"

"I keep normal business hours. I don't have a glamorous job like you." Philip still felt the sting of his conversation with his father.

"Just because I'm not a corporate pirate, doesn't mean I work less than you," Étienne retorted. "I'm a creative. My brain is constantly engaged in the act of composition, which is something even you can't say, boy wonder—"

Philip's snorted, cutting Étienne off. He envisioned his friend, hand on his chest in heartfelt grievance. "Did you call just to rub my lack of work ethic in my face?"

"Never. I called to make sure we were still watching the game."

"What game?"

"Don't you dare," Étienne growled.

"Kidding. I didn't forget."

"Good. Because the last time we had plans, I had to drag you out, with successful results, I might add."

"It wasn't precisely dragging—"

"Monk," Étienne interjected.

"I'm not a monk."

"You're a monk. I'm going to start calling you *Frater Philippe again.*"

"Don't start that."

"I will do as I wish because you know it's true," Étienne answered triumphantly. The game of calling Philip *Frater* went all the way back to their college days, when Étienne had pinned the moniker on Philip during one of his particularly long periods of social withdrawal. "You live like a monk, even though you are young, successful and sometimes, I think, even good-looking."

"I stayed out the whole night with a woman and barely got any sleep. Therefore, I am not a monk." Philip leaned against his desk, smiling at his memory of the evening in question.

"Oh, so did Frater Philipe break his vows with the lovely Val?"

The gleeful shift in Étienne's voice wiped the smile off Philip's face. "No, that's not what I meant—"

"All night, eh? But that is what you said."

"Let me explain—I—we went to her restaurant after we left Aguardiente. I tried her dessert."

"And was she, I mean, *it*, sweet? The dessert, of course."

Philip rolled his eyes. "The tres leches was decadent."

Étienne was merciless. "Don't hold out on me, Frater. Is that all you did?"

Philip nearly growled at his friend. "I spent a chaste night being fed the most delicious sweets and then came home like a perfect gentleman."

"Eh-eh-eh," Étienne said. "You are a romantic, pure and simple. Do not deny it."

An unfamiliar flood of heat raced over Philip's skin. He couldn't be blushing, could he?

"So, are you going to see her again?" Étienne asked.

"We have a date for Saturday."

"A second date? For you, that is practically a relationship!"

Philip changed tack, hoping to sound casual and failing miserably, even to his own ears. "So, uh, what do you know about Val?"

"My lovestruck friend!" Etienne laughed. "I'm sorry to say I don't know very much at all about her, but I can ask Malena. She did insinuate something that she'd heard from…well, you get my drift. I am sharing gossip, so if you want reliable information, you will have to get the real story from your girl."

Warmth and a tinge of something possessive spread through him at Étienne's reference to Val as his girl. "Tell me."

Étienne chuckled. "So impatient, Frater? I think I'm enjoying this."

"Étienne…"

"Only that her last relationship did not end well."

"That I know."

"Do you, now? You must have shared many confidences." Étienne's voice dropped, low and suggestive. "Malena thinks very highly of Val—everyone does, it seems." Étienne paused, but Philip knew more was coming. "But that business with her ex was beyond mortifying. She's not one to be trifled with."

"I don't intend to," Philip retorted.

"Not everyone can be like me," his friend continued, and Philip prepared himself for the requisite self-aggrandizement that always accompanied a conversation with Étienne. "All my ex-lovers are still in contact with me and consider me their friend. Except for Serrano, but he is a special case that we shall not talk about."

Philip snorted. He remembered Serrano and the drama of that breakup.

"There's this thing, though," Philip said when their laughter subsided. "She doesn't know who I am yet."

"What do you mean? She knows your name."

"She knows my name is Philip, some dude with an Alpha Romeo who likes cake in the middle of the night. But she doesn't know I'm Philip *Wagner*, only son of Andreas *Wagner* of *Wagner* Developments."

"Well, it's not like you're Bruce Wayne. Just tell her who you are. What does it matter?"

"It matters, because she thinks my father's company is hell-bent on destroying her neighborhood and she hates us."

"Did she say so?"

"Oh, yeah. She treated me to an earful about it."

Étienne paused before asking, "But how does that affect her? Besides in the philosophical sense."

"She co-owns Navarro's with her father. The restaurant leases the space from the building owners. It's one of the properties my father's after."

Étienne gave a long whistle. "Oh, that's not good at all."

"No, it isn't. Her building is one of the last holdouts, and the acquisitions department has been putting a lot of pressure on the owners to sell. Let's just say, if she could set Wagner Developments on fire, she probably would."

"But my friend, you've got to come clean. Tell her the truth."

"I know." Philip sighed and sank down into his office chair, melting into a mound of dejection. "But I like her."

Étienne's voice softened. "All the more reason why you have to speak up. My mother always says, lies have short legs. Even though I don't know Val, she probably won't take any kind of dishonesty well, if her history is any indication."

"You mean that ex."

"The very same."

Philip's heart sank. "I was thinking of telling her this weekend."

"A good time to man up, Frater. You've got to tell her and take responsibility, yeah?"

"Yeah," Philip answered. "Thanks, man."

There was a rustling on Étienne's side and Philip wondered if the man was still in bed, which would only add insult to injury. "It is already getting late. Order dinner instead. I will bring the beer and we can watch the soccer match at your place, *wi*, Frater?"

The dinging of the elevator beyond Philip's office, together with the slow dissipation of conversation, signified that his father and his investor group were finally gone. "Fine. I'll see you in about an hour."

"Eh, maybe a bit longer."

"Right, because you should at least put your pants on."

Étienne's laughter was crisp and pure as sunlight. "I'm not a monk like you."

"I'm not a monk anymore. I spent a whole night with a woman."

"Eating cake. If you are not careful, you might scandalize the Pope with that behavior. But only the Pope."

Philip ended the call and spun slowly in his chair to face the window behind him. His office looked out over the Manhattan skyline. Small ferryboats crossed and recrossed the river below, while people the size of moving beads lingered on the boardwalk or sped to work in cartoon-sized cars. Alone, on the twentieth floor of the Wagner Building, Philip gave in to his thoughts of Val, which hovered beneath the surface of his preoccupations, an oasis in a desert of calculations and cost analysis.

Philip had good instincts about people. It seemed as though all the things that might make him attractive to someone—his position or his wealth—would matter very little to her. But this situation with his company and the work they were doing in East Ward mattered to her. She had principles.

The same principles that would disqualify him as a potential lover were the very ones that made her irresistible to him. His better instincts should be driving him, the ones that told him to leave her alone, not complicate his project, or her life, by getting involved with her. He really should just cancel the date and delete her number.

But something about Val made him greedy. He liked being around her and wanted to get to know her. But her not knowing who he was would rob her of the opportunity to choose to know him, as well, and that didn't sit right with him. He always faulted his father for his attitude of taking whatever he wanted, consequences be damned. Yet he risked doing the exact same thing with Val.

Lies had short legs, and this one could easily get away from him.

Chapter Five

Tonight's meeting was packed with residents of the Victoria. The chime of the restaurant's front doorbell tinkled over and over until Val finally took it down so it wouldn't interrupt her as she spoke.

"The company has ignored our petitions so far," she began, making sure to pause as Rafi translated. "We are organizing a demonstration outside company headquarters and inviting as many residents as possible to come and make their voices heard. There are extra flyers at the door. Please, take them on your way out and give them to friends and family."

After sharing further updates, Val directed tenants to stations set up throughout the restaurant. Felicia Morales had brought four of her colleagues to consult with residents after the session about their specific situations. Val sat next to Felicia, absorbing the conversations, which were variations on the same theme.

"They raised the rent by twenty percent this year and promised another twenty percent hike next year. I live on my husband's military pension. I've been in my apartment for forty years. How am I supposed to pay the new rent?" Señora Batista, an elderly widow, complained.

Val's blood boiled. She'd played with Señora Batista's grandchildren when she was growing up and spent countless afternoons in the Batista home, dunking toasted Puerto Rican bread slathered with butter and cheese into thick hot chocolate. The widow ran the real danger of eviction from the only home she'd ever known.

Felicia pulled out a business card and handed it to the elderly woman. "Here is an agency that specializes in advocating for veterans and their families. I'd reach out to them."

She thanked Felicia before leaving.

"It's not fair," Val blurted out, giving vent to her increasing frustration. "She shouldn't have to go anywhere at her age. She's been in her apartment since forever."

Felicia placed a warm hand over Val's. "I know, Val. But don't get worked up. Use your anger to effect change. Because you've been so vocal about what's been happening, people respect you and your family. That's a responsibility. Be cool, and it will help others keep their cool, also. As the host, they will take their cues from you."

"So, no keying people's cars? Trashing their offices?"

Felicia laughed. "No car-keying or office-trashing, young lady."

"You're no fun."

Val scanned the familiar faces in her restaurant, each person telling a different story that intersected with her own life. They were her stability, her comfort. After her mother's death, she'd lost all faith in the permanence of things—if you could lose your mother in the space of a single moment, what hope could there be to hold on to anything? These were her people and they had never let her down.

Val's thoughts scattered when her father's friends and the owners of their building, Benito and Eunice Gutierrez, approached. The Gutierrez family had been residents of East Ward long before Val's parents arrived from Puerto Rico. They were Dominican and had taught Val how to make *mangú* and *pastellón* when Val was still in middle school. The Navarros and Gutierrezes had a stronger relationship than just tenant and landlord—they considered each other family.

Eunice pulled Val against her matronly body. *"Hola, mi niña,"* Eunice said, leaning back to pat both of Val's cheeks with her large, calloused hands that smelled of lemon and cumin powder.

Val got up to let the older couple slide into her

spot. She pulled a chair over from a vacant table to sit at Eunice's elbow.

"This is Felicia Morales. You remember—she was at the last meeting."

"Sí." Eunice smiled at Felicia, while Benito shook her hand. "I'm so glad you're here. We wanted to talk to you."

Val reached up and caressed the crucifix between her thumb and forefinger. "Is everything okay?"

Benito looked at his hands as Eunice spoke. "You remember that conversation in the restaurant the other day, *mijita?*"

"Of course," Val answered. Eunice and Benito had shown Val and her father the letters they'd been receiving from Wagner Developments.

"They made us a very good offer and we decided we want to sell the building."

Val's shoulders slumped. Buildings were bought and sold all the time while the businesses renting from them stayed put. However, selling out to Wagner Developments meant the space Navarro's occupied, as well as their apartment, would be owned by a development company that had already demonstrated their lack of interest in the well-being of their occupants when they bought the Victoria.

"Manuel and Emma are hoping we can sell quickly. They want to move out of the city before our granddaughter starts kindergarten this year and we want to go with them." Eunice continued.

Val patted the older woman's arm. "It's natural

that your son would want to raise his family in a quieter place. In the end, it's your property. You have to do what's best for your family." Inside, Val screamed until her brain hurt.

"But you're here to ask my advice, aren't you?" Felicia asked.

Benito pulled letters from a file folder. "We wanted to know if there was a legal way to sell the building while making sure they don't evict anyone."

Felicia shook her head. "Nothing in place right now keeps the company from doing whatever they want once they own the property."

"Criminals," Val muttered.

"There's nothing we can do?" Benito asked, distressed.

"It's why we filed a complaint with the city. Your experience matters," Felicia said. "When we meet with the council, we'll use the collective experiences of the community to get them to give us those protections."

Eunice held Benito's hand. "I'm so sorry, Valeria," she said, sniffling tearfully. "Manuel and his wife don't want to raise their family here and we want to be near the grandchildren."

"There's nothing to apologize for. Do you still want to talk to Papi, or do you want me to tell him?" Val inclined her head toward her father, who was now sitting at a table, talking with a group of old friends.

"We will speak to him," Benito said, getting to

his feet and helping Eunice stand. Val scrambled out of her chair to hold Eunice's elbow on the other side.

"We'll have some more of your cookies. They are so good." Eunice paused, taking Val's face in both her hands again, a habit she'd taken up when Val was a girl.

"You are just like your mother. *Una mujer en pies.*" *A woman with her feet on the ground.* Eunice gave her a kiss on the forehead. "She would be so proud of all of you. Always a positive example to your brother and sister." She released Val's face. "I wish Gabriela had lived to see what a wonderful girl you turned out to be."

"Gracias." Val smiled, though it was hard to keep it in place at the mention of her mother. She hugged Eunice close, willing herself not to cry.

They said goodbye to Felicia and walked away. Val slumped onto her seat and was soon joined at the table by Rafi and Nati.

"Well, that sucked," Val said as soon as the Gutierrezes were out of earshot.

"What happened?" Rafi asked.

Felicia filled them in. Rafi's and Nati's faces slowly went from rapt attention to horror.

"No," Nati whispered.

"It doesn't have to be the end of Navarro's," Felicia said. "It's not in the developer's best interest to get rid of every business in a development zone."

"That's what these guys did in Wagner Financial

Place. All the mom-and-pop stores are gone," Rafi said, his own voice shaking.

"Poor Papi," Nati whispered. "This is his life's work. His and Mami's."

Val drummed her fingers against the tabletop. "You're almost done with school, too. If I could just get you to your graduation—"

"Why don't you guys buy the building?" Felicia interjected. "I always wondered why you didn't own the place by now."

Val stopped tapping the table. "I always wondered that, too. Why didn't Mami and Papi buy the building outright at some point?"

Rafi shook his head. "I don't know." She stared at Rafi, and she knew their minds were spinning in the same direction.

"You're serious," Nati said, her tone of disbelief fading as the possibilities dawned on her.

Val could barely sit still. "I'll call Papi over."

"If you'll excuse me—" Felicia stood "—I'll let you guys talk this one out. If you need any help getting in touch with a mortgage officer, let me know." Felicia made her way to a group at another booth. Val was out of her seat, winding her way behind the counter, where her father was saying goodbye to the Gutierrezes.

"*Con permiso. Papi.* Do you have a minute?"

"*Como no*, I'm going to need a seat after that conversation." he said.

"So they told you?"

Papi's face was serious. "Unfortunately."

He followed Val to the booth where Nati and Rafi were huddled together in deep discussion.

Rafi pulled a chair over for his father. "*Siéntate.* Val has a question for you."

Val glared at Rafi. "Really?"

"You're the eldest," he sang.

"*Pues, pregúntame.* You can ask me anything," her father said as he took the proffered chair.

Val cleared her throat, giving her siblings a pointed look. "We were wondering—why didn't you and Mom buy this building when you first came from Puerto Rico? The Gutierrezes were still renting at the time."

Papi's eyes crinkled the way they always did when they asked him about the past. He loved to talk about when he and Gabriela moved to the mainland, all the hopes and dreams they'd carried with them. "You remember how I told you that my family had a lot of property and used to be rich? We raised all native crops, especially *plátanos* and yuca."

"And you left because the agricultural economy collapsed and your father had to sell everything."

"*Sí.* He divided the inheritance in three parts— one for my parents, one for me, one for my brother. We came to the mainland with that money and put it all in the restaurant."

"There was no chance of buying the building at all?" Rafi asked.

"¡*Muchacho*, no!" He chuckled. "We barely had

enough money to start up the restaurant. By the time we could buy it, the Gutierrezes had bought it, and they weren't letting it go. They raised a family in this building." He shook his head. "I was surprised when they told me just now that they were going to sell it. This would have kept them all the way through retirement."

"Por ese mangansón de Miguel," Val spat. That ruffian of a son, Miguel, who couldn't see past his own interests. Val had never liked him. "He's the reason they're selling."

"Why are you asking me all this?" Papi asked, his eyes flitting toward Nati, who gave him the most ridiculous smile Val had ever seen.

"What do you think if we buy the building from the Gutierrezes?" Val asked.

Papi opened his mouth to speak, then closed it quickly. He glanced at Rafi, who held his hand as if in prayer, and Nati, whose excitement made her look like a bobblehead.

"It's possible," he answered. "But you know how I feel about debt."

She squeezed his hand. "Papi, we should try. Rafi—" she turned her head to take in her brother's giddy expression "—you're the math guy. Do your magical math thing."

"Hell, yeah. If it'll keep the building out of the hands of those vultures."

If they owned the building, Val could ensure the survival of her business, as well as protect her family and the other tenants in the building. She'd be giving Wagner Developments the proverbial finger, and the satisfaction of doing that tasted better than anything she could cook up in the kitchen.

Val was possessed with an inexplicable urge to text Philip and tell him what she was about to do but caught herself before she made that mistake. They were nowhere near that place in their relationship where she should be texting him about something like this. This was a family matter, and she didn't need to bring him into it.

She set her phone aside and instead followed along with Rafi as he jotted down numbers on a sheet of paper, making calculations that would enable them to be independent of Wagner Developments' nefarious plots.

Chapter Six

"Coq au Vin?" Val froze in place, scanning the front of the restaurant as he stepped around to open the car door. "This is so wild. I've heard this place is impossible to get into on short notice. How did you pull off a reservation?"

Philip tucked her hand in the crook of his arm. "I talked to a friend of a friend." That was not entirely true. Wagner Developments owned the property and Philip might have taken advantage of that fact to get the reservation. "I assume, as a restaurant owner yourself, you'd probably appreciate the cuisine. And this restaurant happens to be one of the best."

Val turned her face up to him, her smile outshining the electric lights and lamps along the street. "That's so thoughtful of you. Thank you."

Philip found it nearly impossible to avoid staring. She wore a classic black dress that hung in seductive folds over her curves. She was tall again, though not as tall as the night he met her, the heels of her sandals less precarious tonight. Her hair was pinned in an elaborately braided updo, revealing her long, elegant neck decorated with the rosary from the night they met. A brocaded black shawl hung over her smooth shoulders. He bent his head, his lips a mere hairsbreadth from her ear, and whispered, "You look beautiful."

She shivered in response. "You should speak, dressed like a model."

He didn't think the navy blue blazer, light blue button-up and jeans ensemble he now wore was particularly fashionable, but the compliment warmed him nonetheless. He guided her to the entrance of the restaurant, where the owner manned the host station. Upon seeing Philip, he jumped to attention.

"Nicolas," Philip said. "Ms. Navarro and I have a table for two."

"Very good, sir. Follow me."

Val tugged his arm, pulling him close to her. "He practically threw his back out when he saw you."

"My company holds the lease of this restaurant."

"You own this building?" she asked, scanning the opulent restaurant, with its deep ochre walls, golden lamplight and deep, rich wood.

"Not me personally, I'm afraid." His heart gave a *thump-thump* of terror that she might follow up with further questions, but she appeared distracted by studying the restaurant.

They were taken to the bar, where they would wait for their table to be prepared. Philip waved the bartender over, hoping to head off any more of Val's questions. "White or red?"

"Red," she said, turning her attention to Philip. He nodded to the bartender, signaling that he should fill their glasses.

Val took a sip. "This is very good."

"It's a Bordeaux."

She closed her eyes, savoring the flavor. Her pleasure lit up her face, and Philip forgot the rudiments of drinking and swallowing and…breathing.

She opened her eyes and sighed. "I love a full-bodied red wine."

Philip still held his glass without sampling it, flushed from watching her. "I, uh, I went to a vineyard in Northern Italy once, in the Tuscan region where they make Valpolicella. I stayed in a kind of bed-and-breakfast, and drank from the local cantina. You would have loved it."

"Valpolicella on one hill, Chianti on the other," Val murmured, swirling the liquid in her glass, inhaling the aroma.

"You know your wines."

Val shrugged, her head tilting demurely to the

side. Soft Val was a mood he liked. "I know lots of things." She held her glass out to his. *"Salute."*

"Tchin." He clinked his glass against hers. Val watched him with those glistening eyes, the gears of her brain visibly grinding. Maybe she'd made the connection and his subterfuge was up. However, instead of questioning him, she turned her attention to a small stage where a singer, a tall brunette in a sweeping, silver dress, was singing the strains of "Crazy, He Calls Me" to the accompaniment of a piano.

"Her voice is dreamy," Val said, her eyes on the singer, but Philip couldn't take his eyes off Val. Like the night he'd watched her dance, he was ensnared by the way she gave herself over to the things she enjoyed, desperately wishing he had the ability to do the same. He leaned forward, breathing in her scent, floral and light, and gave himself permission to drag a finger down her cheek with the pretext of moving a wayward curl back into place. Her breath hitched, lips falling slightly open.

"My parents always played music when we were growing up." Val's voice shook but she cleared her throat and continued. "They went through phases— jazz, blues, salsa, disco, rock… You name it, they played it."

"My mother used to play the piano when I was younger." Philip dropped his hand, remembering how her playing filled the high-ceilinged rooms of his family's house where he'd grown up, not entirely sure why she stopped. It never occurred to him to ask her about it. "She's only recently taken up the hobby again."

"When you're raising a family, it's hard to find the time to do what you like."

He let her statement stand. Discussing his family, or his feelings, was something he didn't easily do. Maybe it was because he'd been taught to keep his feelings close, prevent them from exposure for fear they could be used against him. Except here he was, with someone who seemed to define herself by all the ways she connected to others. It was a vulnerable position to start from, but Val was anything but vulnerable. Her heart was out there for the entire world to see. It made hiding himself from her worse because of it.

He forcibly crushed down the guilt, resolving that the night would not pass without rectifying his omission, and concentrated instead on the music and on her.

"There was…there was a record shop where we used to buy LPs." Val's voice had fallen to a rough whisper. "They kept upgrading the technology, but when developers bought out the building, that was the end of Turntable Records." Her hand slid out of his grasp and she took another sip of wine. "Always the same story."

A chill lanced through him, evicting all the warmth her nearness elicited. There it was, again. That compulsion to speak up, to confess. All this did was confirm that if she knew what he did for a living, she would hate him. He needed to come clean, tell her. But the words crammed in his throat, robbing him of his ability to speak.

Nicolas returned to let them know their table was ready.

"Shall we?" Philip asked. Val gazed at him with the same look of curiosity as earlier, as if she were unraveling a snarled riddle. Philip hardly heard the music anymore, focusing the entirety of his senses on the woman before him. Even without his untruth, she was like his personal kryptonite, the temptation to open himself up and lay all his secrets at her feet too great to resist. Whether by weakness or by design, the night could not end without him confessing everything.

Chapter Seven

Val had suspected, from the moment she took a seat next to Philip at Aguardiente that he was doing well for himself. His clothes spoke of style and expensive taste. But it wasn't until he'd opened the door to his black, Italian car to take her home that first night that she came to the realization that Philip might be a little more than well-off. It hadn't been a big deal then. Her aunt Renata, Olivia's mother, wasn't exactly a pauper in her estate outside Lares, Puerto Rico. And her father's family, descended from one of the grand families of Corsica, had been landowners in the nineteenth and early twentieth century.

But when Val and Philip had arrived at Coq au Vin, Val watched the way that Nicolas guy tripped all over himself. They'd simply shown up and waltzed in like royalty. Even now, the waitstaff was scrambling to fulfill Philip's every request.

She liked carrying her fair share of the load in a relationship, but how could she if he had so much more than she did?

Val clenched and unclenched her fists to keep the freak-out at bay and concentrated instead on the pianist who filled the time during the singer's break with an indistinct instrumental piece.

As she struggled with her composure, Philip placed a hand on her back and guided her to a table tucked into the back of the room that gave them an uninterrupted view of the small stage.

The waitress handed Philip the wine menu, which he passed to Val. "You can choose."

She scanned the list, admiring the vintages, until she noticed the prices were missing. She nearly squeaked in surprise but contained it. She'd never dined in a restaurant with no prices, which only meant one thing. She'd probably never be able to afford even half if they split the bill for dinner.

"I think I'll just have water."

Philip watched her, his gaze discerning, though his face remained placid. "Wouldn't you like to try another red? Maybe a Merlot?"

Val bounced her leg so hard, she risked banging her knee against the table. She needed to think quickly. Pretending she didn't drink wine was out of the question—she'd drunk the Bordeaux without blinking. Her thoughts raced until she scooped up the menu, pretending to scan the selections again. "I'll take the house red."

Philip rubbed his chin, considering her for a few moments before taking the wine menu and waving the waiter over. "A bottle of this—" he pointed at the menu.

When the waiter walked away, Val resisted the urge to call him back. The invoice for Nati's classes materialized, as if someone had laid it on the table before her. Lab fees, books, tuition, taxes—a meal like this would cover a good part of that. She couldn't justify it, but here was Philip, asking her to do exactly that. She folded and unfolded her hands on the table until Philip's larger one covered hers, an intense warmth emanating from the contact.

She grasped at the ends of words in a futile effort to tie them together and form sentences. She could make a big deal out of the prices or she could choose to enjoy herself, just this once. It had been so long since she'd done something simply because she wanted to.

When he didn't pull his hand away, she turned hers over and pressed her palm against his. Her anxiety changed focus to the place where their skin met. If his proximity confounded her thinking, his skin against hers short-circuited everything above animal brain functions. Her body surged toward his, the touch of his palm against hers a poor substitute for what she yearned for. She resisted his pull, squirming as delicious aches stole over her.

Before she could get lost, she pulled her hand away and concentrated on the singer, who'd begun another set. The smooth notes soothed her, while the singer's voice possessed an untapped range that filled Val with anticipation each time she approached a high note.

"I like her," she said. "I could listen to her sing all day long."

"She reminds me of Roberta Flack."

"Right?" Val's excitement shook her out of her lust-induced stupor. "Tell me you're a '70s music fan. Please?"

Philip laughed. "If I wasn't, I am now."

Val pulled out her cell phone and opened her Spotify app. "All '70s and '80s, all the time. I would have lived in bell bottoms and platforms."

His eyes were dancing with humor and she decided it was her favorite expression so far. "A fan of the music, yes. The bell bottoms not so much."

"Like I said, my music obsession is my mother's fault. When I said we danced at the drop of a hat, I meant it. My parents used to dance all the time. Over the years, they became flawless."

"Used to? Don't they dance anymore?"

She frowned, the reminder of her mother provoking that ever-persistent sadness that refused to dissipate. She finished the last of the wine to swallow down the feeling.

Philip leaned closer, concern morphing his near perfect face. "I didn't mean to pry."

"No, you're fine. My mother passed away when I was still in high school. So, no, they don't dance anymore."

He gave her a sad smile. "I'm sorry."

Sorry meant pity and she hated pity. "As I was saying," she pushed on. She was on fire and shrugged the shawl off her shoulders onto the back of her chair. "You can tell how long a couple has been together by the way they dance, especially coordinated dances, like salsa. My parents danced like two people who'd been together much longer than they'd been." Val remembered the parties growing up—weddings, backyard barbecues to celebrate birthdays and holidays. Her childhood memories were punctuated by food and music, her parents at the center of every festivity.

When her mother died, the parties stopped for a long time. Val never had a quinceañera because her mother had died that same year and no one had the spirit to celebrate. But when it was Nati's turn, Val made sure she had one.

The silence between them lingered, brittle, full of music and private thoughts. The waiter arrived, filling the emptiness with the sound of wine being uncorked. He poured a careful measure and offered the glass to Philip for sampling, but he demurred, indicating Val.

"You have better taste than I do."

Val pulled a face but accepted the wineglass from

the waiter. She sniffed it, the tart aroma making her nose twitch, and glanced at Philip's expectant expression over the rim of the glass. She took a sip, the wine flowing over her tongue with its heavy, variegated flavor, and knew she was in the presence of a great vintage.

She set the glass down, glaring at him. "This isn't the house red I asked for."

"You're right. It isn't." He nodded to the waiter, who poured two glasses.

"You tricked me." She sounded petulant, though the flavor of the wine softened her indignation, coaxing her forgiveness in exchange for its perfection.

"It wasn't my intention. I just want you to have what you want." He frowned, picking up his glass. "Don't you like the wine?"

He wanted to please her—she could tell by the careful way he studied her reactions. But everything was expensive as hell and it felt positively sinful to indulge in it all, especially when she had to physically resist taking another sip of the extraordinarily rich and sharp wine. She sighed, resigned. "It's possibly one of the best I've ever had."

"Good," he whispered, relief evident in the way his body relaxed. She could make a big deal out of it, go on and on about the expense, but then she'd just come across as annoying and, truthfully, she really wanted to try the food here. Coq au Vin was the kind of restaurant she never thought she'd visit in her life, and now that she was here, she couldn't blow the chance to do so. Plus, there was nothing she enjoyed more than to deconstruct a good meal, something Philip had sensed about her even though he'd known her all of five minutes.

Ay, por favor, who was she kidding? Philip was gorgeous, the music was perfect, the food was probably going to be insanely good and she was dressed to the nines. Locked, loaded and ready. She was going to shut up her inner *bruja* and have herself a good time.

Val was grateful when their *pissaladières* arrived, forcing her to tend to her most banal appetite, pushing the more dangerous ones out of her mind.

For someone as passionate about food as Val, the meal was the equivalent of a visit to a culinary theme park. She ordered artichoke and black truffle soup, followed by toasted mushrooms in truffle oil, a sea-land sampler with buttery cuts of meats and seafood, vegetables in cream sauces, coconut sherbet adorned with bitter cocoa drops and a cheese platter that Val could have made a meal of all by itself.

It didn't help that Philip shared bits of his dishes, as well. She gorged on everything with undisguised glee.

"Had I known cheese would make you this happy..." Philip trailed off in awe. He leaned on his hand, watching her.

"Cheese," Val mumbled around a seasoned olive, all pretenses of delicacy abandoned sometime after the second course. She savored everything using her heightened sense of taste to identify the seasonings used in each dish, filing them away for future experimentation. "Always the cheese."

Philip's laughter was infectious and even the waiter who served them could not repress a smile when he took their order for a digestif.

"I don't know if even the cognac will help, but it was all so good. Thank you."

Philip took Val's hand across the table, squeezing it. "It was worth it to watch you enjoy yourself." He opened his mouth to say more but glanced at the singer instead before giving Val's hand a short tug.

"May I have this dance?" he asked beneath the strains of the singer's rendition of Sinatra's "All the Way."

"I thought you didn't dance," she protested.

"Don't tell Étienne. He'd never let me live it down," he quipped, though it was clear there was more to his aversion to dancing than simple embarrassment.

She took his hand and followed him to the small dance area in front of the piano. When she stepped into his arms, she noticed the panicked rigidity in the way he held her.

"Relax," she said softly, placing a hand on his shoulder and squeezing, thrilling at the muscles bunching beneath his shirt. "Drop your shoulders and lead with your hips."

He glanced between their bodies, observing the way she swayed. Val marveled at how anyone could mess up a slow dance, especially someone who'd supposedly dated a dancer. But he followed her directions, his posture softening, though his feet still did most of the work.

"You have a hard time relaxing, don't you?" Val asked as they swayed.

"I don't come off as uptight, do I?"

Val thought about the way he spoke, so precise compared to her vague, almost careless way with language. It was evident he was used to talking his way around things, revealing just enough and no more than he intended, whereas she, well, she was the equivalent of a verbal hemorrhage.

"Not uptight, exactly. More like guarded. Careful. I don't know you that well, but…"

"That's very observant of you." He stepped back, giving her a slow twirl. She was careful where she stepped to keep from getting her feet trampled by his. "You're right. I'm not a very spontaneous person."

"So do you plan everything?" she asked.

Philip smiled, his eyes thoughtful, and it was like seeing them for the first time, the opaque depths hinting at more than a monochromatic blue. "I didn't plan to dance with you tonight."

"So there's hope for you, yet." She smiled. He was already more relaxed, dancing more easily, though still tense. It would do for now, and she imagined some distant future when she'd take him in hand and teach him to move well. She wanted another night, and another after, and was shocked by the certainty of her desire.

The arm that held her tensed ever so gently and Val followed the subtle movement, stepping closer into the circle of his embrace until they were flush against each other. He might hate dancing, but he was doing it anyway. For her sake. A shiver traveled up and down her spine, landing deep in her belly.

"Am I doing okay?" he asked, his voice thick and gruff.

Her response was to twine her arms around his neck, sinking into the warm knot of his embrace that promised to swallow her in things she didn't dare conceive of yet.

"Let's do this again," he said.

Val took a long, deep breath, the smell of him overwhelming. She hadn't lied. It had been a nice night, but the awkwardness of the expensive dinner hadn't entirely disappeared, and while she'd thrown herself into the experience, it wasn't her intention to be wined and dined. The disparity between them was too much.

"Only on the condition that it doesn't cost a small fortune to go out."

Philip frowned. "Didn't you enjoy it?"

"The dinner was perfect. Flawless, even. But there were no prices on the menu and that probably means you have to take out a small loan to eat here. I…" She bit her lip, trying to fashion the words that would convey her meaning without offense. "I'm not used to that kind of extravagance and I don't want to get used to it."

"What if I want to be extravagant?"

Val brought his face closer to hers. "That's not the kind of extravagance I'm looking for. And it's not the kind I can reciprocate."

"I see," he said, nodding in understanding. "It was a little insensitive of me. I'm just…" He shook his head, and Val's heart softened at his embarrassment.

"You're just not used to slumming it, that's all."

Philip's laughter broke the tension. "I told you. It's not slumming when it's with you. So, a repeat? On a less grand scale?"

She slid her hand down his shirt, his chest warm and hard under her palm, the press of curls rippling beneath the material. Dark blond, like his eyelashes, or a shade lighter, like his hair? Rough and wiry or soft as down? She couldn't help but wonder. She wanted to rest her cheek against his hammering heart until his beat matched hers.

With more composure then she felt, she nodded. "I don't see why not."

He smiled down at her. He was such an intimidatingly well put together man, it was hard to imagine him being insecure about anything. He could ask for whatever he wanted, and between his good looks, his evident wealth and his personality, he'd be assured of getting it.

But in her way, so could she. And right now, she knew what she wanted.

When the set changed, the music morphed into sensuous notes that sent slow currents of longing through her. The low hum of hunger she'd been trying to rein in threatened to break free, demanding to be satisfied. And the way he held her against him, the shattered breathing and wild heartbeat—she knew with unwavering certainty that he wanted to kiss her. It was in the bend of his head, the sudden pliancy of his lips. She tilted her head up and willed him to come to her.

He seemed to follow her silent command, no longer moving with the music. The tea lights on the tables beyond them danced like fireflies, the music cradled them, and he was close, so close, mesmerized as if she were playing a silent tune that drew him in. Val's eyelids grew heavy as his breath unfurled against her lips. But without warning, he pulled back and the moment melted away. Val was shaking, swallowing down both the expectation and disillusion that forced goose bumps to pucker over her skin and ice to flow through her veins.

"You're cold," he said, his eyes still glazed with the remnants of their near kiss, his large hands ghosting over her arms in a rather sensible effort to warm her, provoking a swell of sensation that was both better and worse than her earlier shivers. "Let's get you back to your wrap."

She didn't correct him—how could she tell him that she wasn't chilly, that the tremors he'd mistaken for cold were the double punch of need and disappointment he'd provoked with nothing more than the unfulfilled promise of a kiss?

Dios mío.

As he led her off the dance floor, the voice of caution echoed from somewhere far away, reminding her that it was best she hadn't kissed him, and urged her not to rush this. She had a cascade of betrayals and insecurities at her back, with no need to race headlong into another catastrophe. And yet, for a dangerous moment, she had possessed neither the means nor the desire to stop herself from another train wreck and had been fiercely disappointed that he'd been the one to put the brakes on instead.

Chapter Eight

When Philip eased Val away from the dance floor, he had never been in more need of his natural tendency toward self-control. He'd been close to kissing her, had anticipated the taste and feel of her, and it hobbled his thinking, leaving him in a daze. But just when he was ready to give in, he remembered she didn't know who he really was, and couldn't follow through with the kiss. If she was going to kiss him, it would be Philip Wagner as he really was, not someone she imagined him to be. She had a right to make that decision and she couldn't if he continued to hide his identity. He wanted her to choose to kiss the real him or it meant nothing.

Thankfully, settling the bill and leaving the restaurant gave him the time to cool off and reset to normal. Outside, the night was a perfect intersection of balm and breeze. The path along the waterfront ended at a park that was always windy but the warm evening softened its sting. Val leaned on Philip's arm, the walk clearing away the last of the fog that had descended on him during their dance. They argued briefly about *Star Wars* and laughed at the looks from other strollers at a particularly heated exchange over *The Clone Wars*.

"The only good thing to come out of that was Ahsoka Tano's storyline," Val said, much to Philip's chagrin.

"That's harsh, but you might be right." He glanced past her smile and caught sight of her rosary. "I noticed your rosary the first night we met. It's very distinct."

Her fingers traced the delicate chain. "It belonged to my mother."

She paused in their walk and reached behind her neck to pull the rosary over her head. Taking the crucifix in hand, she turned it over. "See here? On the back? My mother's and father's names and wedding date. And here?" She ran her thumb over the small, silver discs. "There's one each for the three of us— me, then Rafi and finally the baby, Nati, though I'd never survive if she heard me calling her that. Our birthdays are engraved on the back."

She frowned caressing the last, round disk, neatly hidden behind the others. "I had this one made after my mother died. It has the dates of her birth and death. It's not traditional but—" she sucked in a deep breath and handed the rosary to him "—it's my way of making sure she stays present in my life. Otherwise, it's like they die twice when you forget them."

Philip cradled the rosary, examining the onyx beads and silver chain, its fragile weight nevertheless heavy and substantial in his hand. Like her honesty, and his lies. "We shouldn't do that to the people we love."

Val placed a hand on his arm, startling him. "Are you okay?"

He nodded, uncertain. His experience with death was superficial. Relatives died when they were old, after living rather long, full lives. There was mourning and he missed them. But Val's mother had been young, with a family depending on her. Val had dealt with so much, and he didn't want to cause her more pain. He had no right to keep her in the dark about who he really was. His deception had gone on long enough.

Philip looked at her and saw nothing but sincerity in her eyes. She was exactly who she presented herself to be, without filters. Nothing at all like him. "You've been so open with me. So truthful." He brushed a hand over her cheek.

"Philip?" Concern—or wariness—flared across her face. "You've been truthful, as well. Haven't you?"

He took one of her hands. He didn't even have a

right to touch her, but it was beyond his ability to resist. He let her hand fall and held her gaze instead. "Val, what's my name?"

The confusion on her face was painful to look at. "Philip? I got that one minute into our first conversation."

"Philip, what?"

"Philip…" She trailed off, a sheepish expression replacing the confusion of earlier, as if not knowing his last name was something to be embarrassed about, as if he hadn't been the one who'd done everything to keep her from making the connection. "I'm not sure."

"Philip *Wagner*," he said, emphasizing his last name.

Her smile caught him off guard. "That's cool. My name is Valeria Soledad Navarro. If you add my mother's last name, it's Valeria Soledad Navarro-Hernandez. Try saying that fast."

She wasn't getting it. "Val, my name," he prompted, "is the same as my father's company name. Wagner. As in Wagner Developments."

The confusion that stole over her lingered for a few more seconds before it shattered, giving way to a stormy darkness. Her reaction was far worse than he anticipated. "No." She took a step back, bumping up against the railing. "Are you for real?"

"Val—"

"Increíble!" She threw her hands up, scrambling away from him. *"No lo puedo creer. Maldito sea este*

hombre." She pressed the heels of her hands into her eyes and began pacing.

"You're… Val, you're talking too fast." He tried not to crash into her as she paced. "I don't understand what you're saying."

"It's probably better if you don't." She dropped her hands and glared at him. "Philip Wagner? As in Wagner Developments? *That* Philip Wagner?"

"I… Yes, Andreas Wagner's son." He stepped in front of her before she could start pacing again. "But I'm hoping it doesn't change anything."

The wind whipping through her hair gave her a ferocious aspect. "Doesn't change anything? Why should anything change for you? I'm not the one trying to destroy your neighborhood, selling it off piece by piece, leaving people on the streets after they've lived in their homes for years. I'm not the one who lied about who I was." She turned on her heel, striding away from him.

"Val, listen to me." He raced ahead of her, forcing her to come to a stop. "I agree, there are definitely things we can do better. But I'm a designer. You know—I get reports and budgets and I… Val…" She dodged around him and continued down the waterfront walkway at a nearly military clip.

"I still think ignoring the Expanded Universe is a huge waste of lore. I still want to have dessert with you at five in the morning." His longer legs enabled him to outpace her, but she froze, backing away from him with arms crossed.

"Why not just tell me the night we met and save yourself an expensive dinner?"

"I tried. I wanted to tell you."

"Why does that sound a little unbelievable? Maybe you were hoping to find out something you could use to help your project?"

She might as well have slapped him. "I'm not some industrial spy."

"Then why didn't you tell me?" she shouted.

"Because I'm a coward, okay? I was afraid if I told you, you'd leave and I'd never see you again."

"Well, you got the leaving part right, because I'm going home."

Philip's shoulders drooped in defeat. It was late, and even though the streets were full of people, he wasn't going to let her take any risks. "I can't make you stay if you don't want to. But I brought you here and I'll get you back home safely."

Val's lips were pinched thin, her arms still crossed over her chest. He was sure she would turn him down, but to his relief, she acquiesced. "Okay."

They drove back to Navarro's in silence, Val staring out the window for the entire drive, even though there wasn't much to see besides traffic signals and illuminated sidewalks. When he parked under the eternally flickering streetlamp in front of her building, he was sure she'd jump out at the first chance and that would be it. He wouldn't see her again, just as he'd predicted. Her hand was even poised over the handle, as if she was ready to make her break for freedom.

Therefore, he was taken by surprise when she turned to face him instead. "If you go up on the roof of my building, you can see the entire west side of Manhattan, at least up to the bridge. You, more than anyone else, know how much people are willing to pay just to be able to get an uninterrupted view of the skyline."

"I do know." That was the whole point of their work in East Ward. Her town had both the fortune and the misfortune of being located on prime real estate.

"My family came to make a life in this place, despite not knowing the language and being treated like foreigners, even though we're technically as much citizens as you are. I cook and serve food all day. But I get to see the same skyline as you do, even though you're rich and I'm not."

Philip's stomach flipped. But he didn't interrupt her. He could listen, at least.

"That's the dream my parents worked for. The dream for which they gave up everything. It's the dream people like you are destroying."

"That's a lot of responsibility to put on one person."

"It's your company, isn't it? Your family owns it?"

There was no contesting that fact. "I don't know what to say except I wouldn't allow anything bad to happen to you."

"Because you know me? But that's the point, isn't it? Even if it isn't about me, it's always personal to someone."

She turned and stepped out of the car and was at her door before he could answer.

Through the windshield, Philip watched Val push her way in and plod up the stairs to her apartment. Fluorescent lights were never forgiving, mercilessly illuminating every defect.

Yet even in that glare, Val's beauty struck back at the harshness, refusing to be diminished by over-exposure.

Philip had let his cowardice go too far, coloring a complicated situation with a veneer of deceit, something he wasn't sure Val would forgive.

The neighborhood pressed in on his awareness. It was late, but the streets weren't deserted. An older couple stared at him as they walked past Navarro's. What must he have looked like to them, sitting in an idling car, a human cutout against the darkness?

Val's words echoed through his thoughts. He heard fear in every one. She feared for her restaurant. Feared for her home. Feared for the changes to her community. And there was no question. No matter how attracted they were to each other, his was the face of that fear. He was the one bringing these things to her front door.

He put his car in motion and set off, not toward home, but around East Ward. It was difficult to discern what he was looking at in the dark. He was familiar with the waterfront, since that was the location of their prized property—the sprawling factory that they'd start work on as soon as the city approved their plan. The Victoria was next door to Val, part of a block that was strategic to the renovation effort. He knew the demographics of East Ward, the average property values along the different streets and blocks.

But as he studied the darkened storefronts, he realized he didn't *know* East Ward. His father would argue that it wasn't their job to know such things. Their job was to win contracts, maintain a reputation for excellence and turn a profit, a philosophy that he applied ruthlessly to every project he developed. The character of the place was of no consequence to him.

But there were consequences to others. Philip had always been aware of this, but it was easy to ignore in the minutiae of his day-to-day work. He wasn't confronted with this fact when he was working on his designs. They were a game of beauty and symmetry that allowed him to ignore how in the intersections of those gridlines, there were people living their lives. People he couldn't just move around like Monopoly pieces. People like Val who would have something to say about it and would say it loudly.

He was a threat to her and he hated the way that made him feel.

Chapter Nine

Val was running on pure fumes.

Those were her father's words. Ever since her failed date with Philip, Val worked twice as hard to keep from thinking about everything. About him. She arrived at the restaurant at four thirty every morning and stayed as late as she could, or until Nati or Rafi dragged her upstairs. She didn't turn down or delegate any catering jobs, no matter how busy she got. When her evenings were free, she plugged in her earphones and blasted her playlist as she ran until the burn in her muscles forced her back home.

Forget reading her *Star Wars* novel. She had to shove the novel under the bed because it reminded

her of Philip. And thinking of Philip was something
she couldn't afford to do.

Not that it was easy. She was genuinely bummed.
She liked him. He was a little reserved and couldn't
dance to save his own life. But he seemed genuinely nice, and she had a feeling those still waters
ran miles deep.

He'd also lied to her by omission. And he was a
Wagner. What was she supposed to do about that?

"Just delete his number," Olivia said around a
mouthful of pepperoni pizza they'd ordered one
night, as she tried to get through another episode of
her favorite show without getting distracted by her
circular thoughts. "Because that guy right there is
nothing but trouble."

"You're probably right," Val hedged.

"I could create a designer virus. You know, a little
hacker's special, just for my *prima*."

"You are not going to use your programming
skills for evil, you hear me? I'm not bailing you out
of jail when you get caught." Val shoved another
slice of pizza in her mouth to keep from confessing
the truth: deep down, she didn't want to sever ties
permanently. She couldn't stand to think that door
was closed, even if she didn't see a way of stepping
through it. But she couldn't reconcile her desires with
dating her enemy, the person responsible for the frus-
trations, the outright suffering of the people around
her. She couldn't balance the equation.

Instead, she chose to work herself to distraction.

When work wasn't enough, she cleaned. Washed down her kitchen. Scrubbed her floors. Dusted ceiling fans. Polished every piece of wood she could find. When Rafi stumbled on her furiously scrubbing away at the grout in his bathroom, his shout pulled her out of her mindless state.

"¿Pero qué tu haces?" he asked, clutching his chest. "Are you trying to kill me?"

Val wiped the sweat from her brow with the sleeve of her T-shirt. Her hair was wrapped in a bandanna and she wore industrial strength rubber gloves that reached all the way up to her elbows. "I figured, since I was cleaning my bathroom—"

He placed a hand on her arm and gently helped her up from her kneeling position. "Sis, you need to calm down before you end up power washing the whole block."

"Only the sidewalk. And only in front of the restaurant."

Rafi held his hands before him in prayer. *"Ay Dios mío."*

Val crossed her arms over her chest, frowning at her brother. "I might have gone overboard," she confessed.

"You think?" He tugged her out of the bathroom, disrupting her grout cleaning. "Come on. Let's have a little talk."

"Don't you have grading to do?" Val asked, glancing at the pile of papers on his kitchen table.

"I always have grading to do. I grade in my sleep,"

he said. "Some of that is for the mortgage application. It's staggering how much information they want."

"I know. And don't talk about checking all the certificates and permits."

Rafi moved the papers aside. "Sit. *Cuéntame todo.* Tell me everything."

Val pulled off her gloves and rinsed her hands before taking a seat at the table in her father's kitchen, an exact mirror image of her own.

"I'm busy, that's all," Val muttered.

"Your natural default is busy. You know, the normal kind of busy, like anyone trying to run a business. What you've been lately is *maniatica.*" He bustled about the kitchen and, to Val's eternal gratitude, set a kettle to boil instead of making coffee, which would only keep her from falling asleep and make her prey to the thoughts of a certain blond man she couldn't get out of her mind.

Val sat quietly as Rafi placed dried leaves inside a metal tea infuser and poured the boiling water over it. He pulled out the local orange blossom honey that Val loved so much and poured a generous spoonful into Val's cup. When he'd set the mugs down on the table, he took a seat opposite Val. "This wouldn't have anything to do with a certain someone who stopped calling for, oh, I don't know—" he waved his hand in the air in mock questioning "—the exact same amount of time you've been out of your mind."

"We went out once. And I'm not out of my mind," Val protested. "I'm leaving now. Thanks for the tea."

Val stood, collecting her gloves and tea. Rafi put a hand on her arm.

"Val, please. I'm only kidding. You're going through something, baby girl."

No, she wanted to say. Nati and Rafi were her babies. Val was the big sister, the one who should know better than to have problems like this one, the one who should be mature enough to understand that you couldn't always have what you wanted, and that losing was more a part of life than winning. She was the one who had to show them that when they fell down, they got back up, learned the lesson and moved on. She was good at the losing part. The getting back up was always a struggle, and she ended up cleaning every surface in their family's house instead.

All the memories she'd been burying beneath a to-do list the length of the Hudson River barreled into her consciousness. Her and Philip's first—and only—dance. His pigheaded loyalty to the chaos that was the Expanded Universe. How close they'd come to kissing before he pulled away.

"Val!" The sound of her brother calling her name snapped her out of the haze of memories. When she focused on his face, she was struck by how lovely it was. Her father's face, but with his mother's fine bones. Wide-set brown eyes flecked with earthy green. Eyes that now looked at her in concern.

"I'm sorry. I'm a mess." She leaned on her elbows, tugging at her thick curls. "It might have something to do with Philip." She looked up, the compassion in his eyes freeing her. She told him everything, including Philip's revelation that he was a Wagner. She laid it all out for Rafi, finding a measure of relief in releasing her disappointments from the compulsion of her thoughts.

When she'd finished, her brother gave a low whistle. "Damn, girl. Drama just finds you, doesn't it?"

"I'm not dramatic," she said. "I just happen to have a little bad luck."

"You're not kidding. First Luke, and now this. Except Philip was probably minding his own business, doing whatever it is rich people do and then he meets you of all people, so he can't even tell you who he is because he's actually the enemy, and wow, that's the plot of a soap opera."

She would have laughed if she weren't so miserable. "I went out with him one time. What the hell is wrong with me? You'd think I would've learned my lesson." She buried her hands in her hair again, tugging at the strands until tears nearly sprang to her eyes.

Rafi chuckled, dislodging the bandanna that held her mane in place, and with it, her hands. "Are you trying to go bald? Look, you like him, that's your problem. But even though he's good or what have you, he also happens to be the one guy you do not need to be thirsting after. This situation's got you turned out."

She sat up, snatching her bandanna from him. After a few half-hearted attempts to tame her hair, she let the curls fall free. She was sure she looked like some mad island spirit. "You're right. I mean, he's out of my league anyway."

Rafi wrinkled his nose as if he'd caught a whiff of something rotten. "Out of your league? *You're* out of *his* league. You're the one trying to do right by everyone else. He can't even tell you who he is, and when he does, come to find out his company is the one causing all the trouble. You are gold, sis. You don't need any part of that."

Val melted. "You think I'm gold? That's so sweet."

Rafi ruffled her messy hair. "Don't let it get out. I have to keep up my reputation as a badass."

Val giggled. Rafi was about as threatening as a pug. "You're right, though. I don't need any part of that."

"Mmm-hmm." Rafi scanned her up and down, like he didn't believe a word she said. "But, let's just say for the sake of argument you did want a part of that action," Rafi said slowly. "He'd have to do something to show you what he's about. Because no matter what you guys feel for each other, it's his company causing problems."

That was the crux of it. If Val didn't care about her community, she could ignore the consequences of Wagner Developments' project for everyone she knew and just follow her attraction to Philip.

But she did care. This time, she really couldn't have everything she wanted.

"I noticed your baseboards are looking a little dusty," Val said.

Rafi put his head in his hand, groaning in response.

Chapter Ten

"Have you been outside today?" Andreas asked without preamble when he walked in and took the seat across from Philip's desk. Philip had his hands full with the new project proposal for a large-scale industrial complex in Syracuse and it hurt his head to break away from it.

"I've been a little busy."

"Take a look." Andreas gestured toward the office window. Philip rose from his chair. Even from his distant vantage point, he could see a large group of people on the sidewalk outside the building, holding signs. It looked like they were chanting, though he couldn't hear it from where he stood. He squinted at the boulevard separating their building from the waterfront.

"Is that a news truck?"

Andreas sank into the chair across from Philip's desk. "I'm afraid so. They think public shaming is going to work on me."

Philip had no idea what he was talking about. His father huffed at his confused expression.

"A community group has lodged a formal complaint with the city, temporarily blocking our project in East Ward's opportunity zone. We're fighting it, of course." He leaned back, gripping the arms of his chair in obvious frustration.

It sounded like the kind of thing Val would get involved with. "Wouldn't it be worthwhile to see what the complaints are about before deciding you're not going to work with them?"

"I sent Leighton to get rid of them. Protests are bad for business." George Leighton was the head of the company's legal department and knew better than anyone what the company was allowed to do.

"Sending a lawyer to speak for us is a bad look. You should go, too."

"But I am within the boundaries of the law, so there is nothing to discuss."

"It wouldn't be out of the ordinary to arrange a meeting to discuss the complaints. Maybe have PR announce the meeting to the media as a show of good faith—"

Andreas scoffed. "Good faith? That's your mother's area of expertise." He picked imaginary lint from his immaculate trousers. "This is a business, not a charity."

Philip's breath was coming hard now. "I don't see how running good PR translates into charity."

"It comes from a sentimental place, an approach not suitable for business."

His father always did this. Always made Philip feel like he'd been made from a defective blueprint. He'd grown accustomed to his father's impossible expectations, how tied to his affections they were, and learned to ignore how that fact hurt him.

If Andreas noticed—or cared—about Philip's rising temper, he gave no indication. "If either of us goes out there, it will look like a capitulation and I won't be seen to do that. Protest or not, this project will come to fruition."

"You're not listening," Philip said, his head suddenly heavy. "We have a whole department dedicated to interacting with the community. Why wouldn't you use them?"

Andreas paused at the threshold on his way out. "If you're so concerned about it, you take care of it. As long as you make them disappear."

"And you'll consider listening to their complaints?"

"You can feel free to listen to their complaints. I have a company to run." With that, he walked out.

Philip pinched the bridge of his nose. His father was exhausting sometimes. Everything would be so much easier if his father would simply allow a new idea into his head, but listening and admitting he was wrong were two things he seemed constitutionally unable to do.

Philip took the elevator to the ground floor and

stepped out into the familiar atrium, a vaulted glass and metal entryway designed to inspire awe for its pristine futurism. A towering tree embedded in a faux spring stretched upward into the open space, three stories high, a nod to the ecological efficiencies and elegant aesthetics of Philip's designs.

George Leighton, a diminutive man whose entire demeanor screamed *polish*, was deep in conversation with a younger woman Philip didn't recognize. Philip pulled him aside. "Who is that?"

"She's an intern from Media Relations."

Philip pinched the bridge of his nose. "An intern? Don't we have anyone more experienced? What about a community liaison? Someone who's had contact with this group before."

Leighton shrugged. "Mr. Wagner suggested that anyone in PR would be able to handle communications with community reps, so we don't actually have a community liaison."

"Well, obviously, not just anyone can do the job, otherwise there wouldn't be protests outside our door. I don't want an intern anywhere near this project after today. We need a designated liaison and we need to appoint them as soon as possible."

Leighton, to his credit, said nothing, calling over the young woman and quietly dismissing her to go back to her office.

"I'll take over until then." Philip indicated the group outside. "Who is their organizer?"

Leighton gestured toward the crowd. "Felicia Morales is a housing advocate and lawyer with the East

Ward Fair Housing Coalition. She's a familiar player in this community's activism."

Philip followed Leighton's gesture and saw the woman in question. Tall, dark-haired, she held a colorful, hand-painted sign that had the company name covered with a red circle and backward slash. But it was her companion who sucked all his attention away.

Surprise twisted in his chest at the sight of Val, holding her own sign, deep in conversation with Morales. Surprise combined with the effect she always seemed to have on him, made worse by the conviction that he thought he'd never see her again. Of course, she'd be here. She was the cofounder of the organization. If his revelation of being a Wagner had been enough for her to leave him on the side of the road, then he should have anticipated she'd be a participant, if not leader, of a protest like this.

She was irresistible, especially now, with the flush of excitement coloring her cheeks. Her hair was tied back and, even in jeans and her restaurant T-shirt, she was as magnetic as she'd been the night they met.

"Are you ready to speak to them?" Leighton asked.

Philip started at the sound of his voice. "Yes… yes, of course."

He tugged at his tie, hoping Leighton hadn't picked up on his distraction. While going slack-jawed over a woman was not unheard of in the history of humanity, he should probably not do so in front of his employees.

Chapter Eleven

Val delivered her prepared statement and answered questions from the local news crew, making sure they understood that Wagner Developments had so far been unwilling to communicate with community leaders on their demands for fair housing, driving them to picket outside the company headquarters to raise awareness and to follow by filing a formal complaint. A heady rush of empowerment accompanied the wrap-up of the interview, the euphoria of knowing that all the planning and organizing of the past few months were finally yielding something concrete.

"You're a natural, Val," Felicia said proudly. "You'll see. They'll have to pay attention to your demands, if only to save face. Corporations like this hate bad publicity, almost as much as they hate delays in their project schedules. And we hit them with both."

"Doesn't it sometimes seem like all we're doing is throwing pebbles at a mountain?" Val said.

"David slugged a stone at Goliath, and you saw how that turned out."

Val smiled, but it melted when the glass doors of Wagner Developments' headquarters swished open and out came the star of her every dream, tall and handsome and treacherous as always. She'd entertained the possibility that she might see him, though she thought it a remote one. He was a designer, a job that didn't require him to interact with the public. She wasn't prepared for his appearance and found herself unable to tear her eyes away. He was accompanied by another man, but he was of zero interest to her. She was glued to the way Philip moved, how his suit, with its modern cut and almost too-snug style, molded itself to his body. Probably tailor-made for his wide shoulders, narrow waist and legs that didn't know when to quit.

Legs she shouldn't be ogling like some sex-starved spinster.

Of course, someone else hadn't gotten the memo, either. The memo that said you shouldn't show up at someone's protest, especially if you were the target of said protest, looking like you'd stepped off a runway. Philip's face was impassive but his gaze was all over her. Val put up her sign between them.

Not today, *Señor Diablo*.

"Val," he said, his voice cool and measured. "It's good to see you again."

"You've met?" Felicia asked.

"Only…that one time in Aguardiente…" She trailed off. She wasn't technically lying. They'd met. That one time. In Aguardiente.

"Well, that helps," Felicia said, side-eyeing Val strangely. "Felicia Morales. I represent the community in East Ward. Your company has been remarkably unresponsive to us."

"I'm George Leighton, Wagner Developments' General Counsel. Maybe we should we step inside," the man next to Philip said, eyeing the news truck and the chanting crowds. He probably hoped they wouldn't catch wind of them talking and come back over again.

"Actually, I'd like to make arrangements for a more formal meeting. It really shouldn't have gotten to this point, and I apologize for that," Philip said smoothly.

Val raised an eyebrow. "It's not like you don't have a way to reach out to me…us," Val self-corrected, catching the look of surprise on Philip's face. "We've been trying to speak with a representative for months now."

"We'll just remind him again of how to reach us," Felicia said slowly, looking from Val to Philip before handing him a business card she'd fished out of her bag. "That is, if we have someone who might actually return our calls."

"I'm confident the communication will be as open

as you want it to be from now on." He gave Val a pointed look, as if the words were meant for her and only her before turning his entire attention on Felicia. "Val gave me a preview of the situation when we spoke. Maybe we can resolve this without a hearing."

"Good to know. We'll be in touch," Felicia said, deliberately noncommittal. She was right not to be persuaded by anything Philip said without proof of his commitment. But he sounded so amenable that Val almost dared to hope that their protests might have yielded something positive, that Philip might be acting out of a sense of human decency. Which was downright delusional on her part, because Philip was a Wagner, and his company was only cooperating with them because they were under the threat of losing money and looking bad.

She had to stop allowing herself to be carried away by the desire to see good intentions in people where there weren't any. She did it with Luke and now she'd almost done it with Philip.

"Thank you," Felicia said.

"And perhaps—" Leighton indicated the crowd around them "—your work is done here?"

"We were scheduled to end now anyway," Val answered. "You see, we are willing to work with you as long as you're willing to work with us."

"I think you'll be pleasantly surprised at how willing we are to work with you," Philip answered, his gaze pinning her in place. He spoke as if everything he said had a second and third layer of meaning.

She glanced around to see if she was the only one who sensed this. It made her feel vulnerable and she didn't like it one bit.

Without acknowledging Philip, she turned away to speak to the group of protestors and thank them for coming out, promising them they'd meet again to debrief and plan next steps. Val sensed the weight of Philip's eyes on her, but she didn't turn to confirm if she still held his attention. She wanted nothing more than to escape back to the familiar safety of her restaurant, her home and her people, where thirst-traps like Philip couldn't get to her.

"How could you not tell me you met Philip Wagner?" Felicia said as they stuffed signs in the back of Val's delivery van. Val should have known better than to think Felicia was going to let all that go without comment.

"I… It was a social thing. I didn't even know who he was the first time we met."

"The first time?" Felicia crossed her arms, looking Val up and down. "How many times have you two met?"

Val wanted to punch herself in the mouth. "Just… twice."

Felicia stared at her. Val continued putting the signs in the van, arranging them in size order, as if that would make any difference once the van was underway.

"Listen, your personal life is your business," Felicia said, waving a finger between them. "But this thing we're doing here is a partnership. I need to know these little details, like when you go out on a date with the son of the owner of the company you are protesting against, or I can't be effective in helping you."

Val slammed the doors of the van with more force than necessary. "As soon as I found out who he was, I cut things off, so there didn't seem to be anything to tell."

Felicia put her hands up as if Val was threatening to mug her at gunpoint. "I'm not saying you did anything wrong. I just need you to communicate with me."

Val didn't think she'd done anything wrong, either, but the whole thing weighed on her all the same. She climbed into the cab, Felicia buckling in next to her. Val hoped she was done talking. The encounter had been cringey and Val looked forward to stuffing the events of the afternoon into a corner of her mind and ignoring them, along with everything else Philip-related.

After they got underway, Felicia asked, "You haven't mentioned to him your interest in buying the building, have you?"

Val looked over at her. "Of course not. I would never give him, of all people, that kind of information."

"Smart girl." Felicia grew quiet, much to Val's relief. But it was short-lived. "I will make one observation, though."

Val gripped the wheel more tightly, not particularly eager to hear that observation. "Go ahead."

"He didn't seem…indifferent to you."

Val scoffed. "Oh, please. It's been almost two weeks since we went out. I'm surprised he remembers my name. Anyway, he's not my type."

Felicia shrugged. "He might not be your type, but it's pretty clear you're his."

Val scowled but didn't say anything more. She left Felicia at her office before returning home. Nati had rotations at the hospital and wouldn't be back for a few hours, for which Val was grateful. It meant she could pace to her heart's content. Val couldn't think unless she was moving.

She reviewed the events of the afternoon, unable to make sense of them. Wagner Developments had been ignoring them for months, using every possible ploy to avoid a meeting with community leaders until they'd been forced to go to City Hall and lodge a formal complaint against them.

Then today Philip Wagner, of all people, shows up with his "you'll be pleasantly surprised at how willing I am to work with you" shtick, as if his company had been waiting for a chance to do something all along.

It made no sense.

If only he knew how much she despised surprises. The last surprise she'd received had been the one Luke sprung on her, and she wasn't keen on receiving any more. She needed to know what Philip was up to, though she doubted he'd simply offer up a confession just because.

She pulled out her phone and scrolled through her contacts until she found Philip's number. Without pausing from her pacing, she pressed the call button and listened as the phone rang. She expected, as busy as he was, for him to not pick up. But after the fourth ring, he did.

"Val," he said, the pleasure evident in his voice, but also the curiosity. "What a surprise. It's really great to hear from you."

She wanted to say likewise, because it *was* good to hear his voice, but that was a bad idea, even if the sound made her feel like she had a can of fizzy soda in her stomach. "So, what was today all about?"

He didn't answer right away, which meant she'd probably caught him off guard. Good. "You're the one who came to protest outside my building."

"Obviously. What I mean is, what's the deal with you? First your company refuses to meet, barely bats an eye at the complaint we filed. Then you show up, the picture of benevolent cooperation. What are you up to?"

His laugh had the combined effect of grating on her nerves and kicking her heartbeat into overdrive. "I'm not up to anything. You have legitimate concerns, and I want to do something about them."

"Just like that?"

"No, not just like that. It makes good business

sense to work with the communities where we have projects."

Val had nothing to say to that. Really, what had she expected? That his company had decided to co-operate because of her? Because he liked her so much that he'd become more virtuous? That wasn't a healthy thing to want.

"Why didn't you guys do it in the first place?" she asked.

Philip sighed deeply. "I didn't know there was a complaint. But I should have and that's on me. I tend to have a very narrow focus when it comes to my area of expertise. But that's not an excuse and I apologize for that."

"Right. Okay," she said. "I hope you're serious about a compromise because a lot of people are de-pending on this going well."

Philip's response came slow and clear. "Val, there is nothing I take more seriously than my work. My father is a little old-school when it comes to the re-lationship between development and the communi-ties he works in, but times change and our company will evolve, as well."

Val nodded, almost convinced that he might be telling the truth. "If you're acting in good faith, then that's all I can ask."

"I appreciate the vote of confidence," he said. "How is your culinary empire?"

Val found herself pacing again. They were doing

small talk. She could handle this. "Oh, you know, sucking the life out of me as usual."

"And yet you love every minute of it."

"Without any doubts." She guessed it was her turn to volley something in return. "Your car? Is Étienne taking care of it?"

"Ah." He laughed and fizzy bubbles spread through her chest, forcing a shiver from her. "That scoundrel just got back in town after being gone for two weeks and my car spent the entire time in the garage. It's no wonder she loves him more than she loves me."

"Maybe because you work too much. You should take her out more often."

"I like company when I drive." His silence was heavy with suggestion, but Val knew better than to play into it.

"My ride is a twenty-year-old, refurbished catering van," was her response.

"Is that what you take on your *Fahrvergnügen*?"

"A who?"

"It means 'pleasure drive' in German."

"I'm going to have to apologize in advance because my van speaks only Spanglish, and there is no pleasure involved in driving her." Val couldn't believe she was allowing herself to have a normal conversation with Philip.

"All I can offer you is a ride in a temperamental Italian car that is resolutely monolingual."

Val gasped. "Did you just invite me for a car ride?"

Philip laughed again and it was having a dangerous effect on her. This whole conversation was going sideways. "Sorry. I got carried away. Spoiler alert, I like you. But if you don't feel comfortable seeing me socially, I understand."

"You're right. I don't feel comfortable seeing you socially. It would be a massive conflict of interest," Val retorted.

"I respect that." He came off so agreeable, Val didn't know if it was just an act or if he was being sincere. But he had real power, and if he was really motivated by a desire for change, he might simply need a nudge to do the right thing. Val believed in giving people a chance to step up, and she could offer that to him.

"You know, it might help both our causes if you got to know my neighborhood. I know East Ward better than anyone."

"Are you offering to give me a tour?"

Val stopped pacing again, her breath coming hard, even though she wasn't exerting herself at all. "I'm offering you the opportunity to become better informed about the community you are impacting."

"And this isn't a social encounter."

"Absolutely not." Val waved her hand, even though it was impossible for him to see the gesture. "It's raising awareness. As in me raising your awareness."

She steeled herself at his pause, but thankfully, it didn't last long. "Okay. Message me the best day and time for you and I'll make it work."

"I would think your schedule might be more hectic than mine."

"I'll move things around if I have to," he responded without hesitation.

Val sank slowly into the pillows of her love seat. "This is important to me."

"I know it is. Consider it done."

She didn't overthink his motives. She might regret it, but she chose to believe that this was something that mattered to him, as well. "Thank you."

The small huff she heard on the line sounded like a laugh, soft and natural, without any affectation on his side. "I'm so glad you called."

Val didn't know what more to say, so she said goodbye and hung up. She glanced up at a small painting of a *flor de maga*, the red hibiscus that was also the national flower of her family's island. Bright and swollen with color, fragile as crepe paper. The way Val felt. If a breeze came in too hard, she might crumple up into a ball. The day had been a lot and she had reached her saturation point.

As she prepared a bath, the only thought that returned to her was that she had called Philip and she had invited him to tour her neighborhood. She could choose to question his motives, and she definitely did not trust him. But she knew if she looked a little more closely at her own motives, she would discover that they were not as pure as she wanted them to be. And that was a problem of another order of magnitude.

Chapter Twelve

After Philip's conversation with Val, he was too excited to work on his project, and he knew he wasn't getting anything else done. He couldn't believe the turn events had taken. This morning, he was just plugging away as usual at one of his designs, focused entirely on solving technical issues in the plan. Then Val came along and blew up all his concentration, first with the protest and now with this neighborhood tour.

It wasn't a date, she'd said. It was work. But there was no way to convince his nerves of the distinction.

Étienne had only just returned from another one of his photoshoots, barely even cleared airport security, but Philip was already on the phone, hoping he'd be up for a game of tennis.

"You hate tennis," Étienne said. He wasn't wrong. Philip's father had insisted that he learn to play golf and tennis so he'd be in a position to play with clients in a business capacity, even though neither was his preferred sport.

"But you don't. And I already reserved a court."

"I have been sitting for hours," Étienne said thoughtfully.

Philip looked around at his office, feeling zero motivation to return to work. "I need to get out of here."

"Needy boy," Étienne said. "What time?"

An hour later, Étienne arrived on the court, decked out in one of his signature outfits—crisp, white shorts and a snug white-and-lime-colored sports shirt that brought out the undertones of his dark skin. He looked like he'd stepped out of a *Sports Illustrated* advertisement for Wimbledon and was strutting like a model.

Philip looked down at his well-used Nike sneakers, mismatched shorts and T-shirt and realized he didn't even qualify for the fashion competition.

"Frater!" Étienne called from across the court, tossing a bright yellow towel over his shoulder. "Did you borrow those shorts from your father?"

"No, they're yours."

Étienne's horror pulled a laugh from Philip. "I refuse to claim them."

"Okay, sure. Which side of the court do you want to start on?"

"Doesn't matter, since I will thrash you either way." Étienne pointed with his racket to the opposite end of where they stood. Hedges lined the court, shielding them from view of other players and passersby.

"Dreaming big? Just serve."

Étienne obliged, sending the ball hurtling toward Philip for a warm-up before they began playing in earnest. The exchange was punctuated by the satisfying snap of the tennis ball against their rackets. Philip wasn't in love with tennis, but it was a sport that required his total concentration, which helped to clear the thoughts that had cluttered his mind since his conversation with Val. Sweat ran down his forehead, while Étienne played with perfect equanimity until he scored the winning point of the set.

Étienne tossed a bottle of water to Philip before uncapping his and taking a long drag. Étienne had soundly thrashed him but he was grateful for the calm provided by the physical exertion.

"Do you remember Val Navarro? From that night you dragged me out to East Ward?"

"How can I not? She almost deflowered you before casting you aside."

"Leave it to you to make everything sound like a soap opera," Philip retorted over Étienne's laughter. "Seriously. She was protesting today outside Wagner Towers."

Étienne stopped chortling. "Uh-oh."

Philip filled him in on their conversation, though

he kept a few things to himself: The flash of recognition in her eyes that had been more than just shock. The quick recovery before she blew him off as if they hadn't shared a connection. And how much that false indifference had grated on him.

"And you know, I get it. In her mind, when she looks at me, all she sees is who I work for." Philip placed his hands on his hips, looking up into the clouds as if an answer to his problems might fall like a brick from heaven and land on his face.

"You're not your company. And you are certainly nothing like your father. You're different. You always have been, or I wouldn't be able to tolerate you," Étienne said as he crossed the tennis court. "But she doesn't know that, because she doesn't know who you are."

"I'd like to change that. I have never been in a situation where my very existence is a direct threat to anyone." Especially someone he could come to care for.

"She feels threatened because she is at a significant disadvantage with respect to you."

"But I'd never take advantage of her."

Etienne clapped a hand on Philip's shoulder. "That might be, but from her perspective, she is in a precarious situation. It may be difficult for you to grasp how that might make her feel because, and excuse me for saying so, you've never been poor."

Philip made to speak, but Étienne put up a hand to stem his protests. "Listen, okay? You don't have the experience of being at the mercy of forces that neither see, understand, nor care about you. Like being in the hands of an angry Loa. Or buried alive by an earthquake."

Philip was flooded with both admiration and shame. Étienne had experienced total powerlessness when the Great Earthquake forced his family to flee Haiti, overturning his life. "I don't know what it's like. But you do. It must have been terrible."

"Yes, it was. It is difficult to forget," Étienne pitched an imaginary ball into the air to practice his serve. He was graceful and elegant, the powerful muscles of his body stretching up to maximize the motion. "It conditions everything you do."

Philip rubbed his chin, his mind whirling away. "I don't need to have experienced it to imagine how hard it must be."

Étienne placed a gentle hand on Philip's shoulder. "And because I know you, I know this to be true, as well. But I repeat, she does not. And she has a very legitimate fear, given what's been happening in East Ward lately."

"That's Dad being…Dad. You know how pig-headed he can be. We don't even have a community liaison in-house. He just thought he was going to go into East Ward, bulldoze over everything and create it anew in his image."

"Papa Andreas says, 'Let there be light.'" Étienne's laugh was a sober one. He had experienced the phenomenon that was Andreas Wagner many times in their years of friendship.

"She invited me to tour her neighborhood with her."

Étienne froze in his movements. "Really?" He straightened. "But you just said—"

"She called me, trying to figure out what I was up to and the conversation led to that."

Étienne resumed bouncing a ball on his racket. "Clever Val. It makes sense. But what are your intentions?"

"What do you mean?"

"You're not doing all this just to get with her?"

"No, it's not only for her." Philip tossed the tennis ball from one hand to the other. "I don't like feeling this way."

"What way?"

"Like I'm not…worthy. Like what I do is so intrinsically damaging that a person with even half a conscience doesn't want anything to do with me because of it. I don't want to be that person."

"You're not that kind of person."

"Aren't I, though? For the first time, possibly ever, I've finally met someone who is not only intelligent and fun to be with, but principled and decent, as well. The whole package. And that person doesn't want anything to do with me because I am an active danger to everything that matters to her. And not just to her. There were more than a hundred people at that protest. To them, I am that kind of person. My company is that kind of company."

"What's your plan? Are you going to take on your father?" Étienne asked.

"He didn't want to meet with the protesters but I did. I pushed and he gave in. He knows as well as I do that Wagner Developments is going to be mine someday. It's time I act like it."

Étienne tapped his chin thoughtfully, observing Philip. "No more hiding behind your fancy designs? It's all very Henry V, you know? Boy prince who reluctantly embraces his throne."

"I've never been reluctant about my work."

Étienne shrugged. "I happen to know that, if you truly wished it, you could do anything you want with that company. Your father might resist you every step of the way, but he would not deny you, if only because you are his heir. You love your designs, it is true, but you use them to shield you from the more unpleasant parts of your work, like facing community complaints."

That hit its mark. Étienne was right, but telling him so would make him unbearable. Philip laughed instead. "Maybe. Except Prince Hal is much more debauched than I've ever been."

Étienne accepted the feint. "I agree with you, Frater. You are quite boring."

"Just for that, I'm going to wipe the court with you."

Étienne laughed his full-hearted laugh as he took

up his position. "Always the same last words. At least no one can say you don't have practice losing."

Philip responded to Étienne's serve, dwelling on what his friend had said. He wanted to spend time with Val, get to know her, wherever that led. But he wanted more than just to have her. He wanted to earn Val's respect, for her sake, but also for his own.

Chapter Thirteen

Philip wiped his sweaty palms against the leg of his jeans. Val had asked him to stop by at 6:30. Now he was here, at 6:21, sitting outside her building and channeling his inner stalker. With restaurant lights switched off, the darkness of the shop became a forbidding presence staring back at him.

"I can wait," he murmured, trying not to stare at his phone, all the while staring at his phone as the longest nine minutes of his life ticked by. Waiting finally got the best of him at 6:27 and he found himself crossing the street.

He was brought up short by a man who stood before the closed door, the sound of the buzzer indicating he was being let in. He was tall and muscular, with auburn hair that fell in long waves over his collar. Philip took the opportunity to slip in behind him.

When the man turned to glance at him, Philip pretended to stand at the mailbox, checking for letters. Luckily, the man lost interest, and, as nonchalantly as possible, Philip waited until he was a flight ahead of him before taking to the stairs. He expected the man to continue past Val's floor, so it was a surprise when he came to a halt before her door instead.

Philip slowed his steps. The man ran his fingers through his hair before knocking on the door. Philip's heart skipped when it opened and Val appeared on the threshold.

"I was expecting somebody else. What do you want?" she said in a voice Philip had never heard her use before. She was as beautiful as always with her curls pushed back under her bandanna. She wore her stained red shirt with the white lettering of Navarro's Family Restaurant printed across the front and faded blue jeans with tears above the knees. She also sported a scowl that could melt the paint off the walls.

The man cocked his head to one side, and though Philip couldn't see him, he imagined his eyes raking over Val. Philip repressed the urge to march up the remaining stairs and toss him over the railing, but kept his place instead. The man's voice dripped with sweetness. "Don't be like that, baby."

Baby? The impulse he'd held in check morphed into something hateful. He clutched the banister but waited. This was Val's business, not his, and he needed to let her sort it out.

"Be like what? Why are you here?" she retorted.

"I was in the neighborhood and wanted to see you."

Val rolled her eyes before settling her glare on him again. "You saw me. Now you can go."

"Just hear me out. I want to clear up a few things." He stepped closer, too close. Val scowled more fiercely, lifting her chin in defiance. Philip admired her courage, but she didn't stand a chance against someone that size. Hell, *he* might not stand a chance against someone that size.

"Now? After eight months? Now you want to drop in for a little visit and say hello?"

Was this the infamous Luke?

"I think I and everyone else in Aguardiente have heard enough from you," she continued. "You told the world you were playing with me, that I was just a little side adventure and that the real party was the lady you were living with the entire time you were with me. I don't need to see you or hear another word from you."

"Can't we take this inside?" He was now almost nose to nose with her, so close, she had to lean back to keep him out of her personal space. Philip took the last few steps two at a time until he was next to Luke.

"Hey, sorry I'm late, sweetheart. Traffic was insane." He left a quick peck on Val's cheek. Her wide eyes and surprised expression were the answer to his own maniacal smile. He turned toward Luke and stuck his hand out. "I'm Philip. Nice to meet you."

Luke slowly shook his hand. He was shorter than Philip, but his physical presence was solid.

"Luke," he said, his voice a low baritone that promised dangerous things.

Philip shook the man's hand with a strong grip, holding it a beat longer than was polite. He remembered his father's lesson on handshakes—be the first, shake the hardest, hold the longest. It was the polite equivalent of peeing on a tree to mark your territory but it had served Philip well in life. When he let Luke's hand go, he watched the man flex his fingers.

Having made his silent point, Philip turned away as if Luke no longer existed and handed Val the flowers. "Ready to go out?"

A smile hovered at the edge of Val's lips, though her face remained stern. "Yeah. I just need a few minutes to clean up." Her happy eyes and the softening of her features were a sharp contrast to the bulldog face she'd pulled on Luke only a few minutes earlier.

Take that, you jerk.

She turned back to Luke. "I have plans tonight. Don't come by again without calling first."

She took Philip by the hand and tugged him inside. He was aware that he was allowing himself to be used, but her touch brought back their moment on the boardwalk before everything had gone to hell. It seemed like a hundred years ago, and he was hungry for any crumb that Val flung his way.

Graciously, Luke tipped his head. "I get it. I'm too late." Philip gave him his most bored expression. Luke's discomfort was so palpable, Philip almost felt sorry for him.

Val lifted her chin again and nodded once. Luke waved at Philip before turning around, descending the stairs with a speed that belied his bulk. Val leaned against the doorjamb and took a long, noisy breath. She gave Philip a searching look, as if she was debating whether to throw him out as soon as she gathered her strength again.

Instead, she stepped aside, sweeping a hand in the direction of the living room. "Sorry you had to see that. Come in."

Philip didn't hesitate. He entered, inhaling her smell—cooking spices, coconut, perhaps from her conditioner, and an undertone of something feminine and musky, the delicious aroma that belonged only to Val.

She shut the door before following him to her living room. "Can I get you something to drink?"

Her voice didn't possess its usual warm timbre and he missed that. He realized he was staring at her and tore his eyes away.

"Don't trouble yourself."

"Well, I'm thirsty so have a seat." She turned and slipped into the small kitchen, and he heard the sound of a refrigerator opening. Philip was too excited to sit so he took in the apartment instead. Like the restaurant, it was small but cozy. A rust-red sofa with giant, perfectly arranged pillows took up most of the space. The walls were painted in soothing beige tones except for a cappuccino-colored accent featuring built-in shelves stuffed with Star Wars novels.

Val took a seat on the sofa, fixing her eyes on him. A mask had fallen over her features, the flicker of friendliness buried deep where he could not reach it. He wondered if it was because of the scene with Luke he'd just witnessed. She was a proud woman and probably didn't appreciate being confronted by an ex on her doorstep.

Philip took a seat next to her. Her face twisted, and he realized she was biting the inside of her cheek.

"I had Luke all under control."

"I know. You're perfectly capable of taking care of yourself. I just wanted to make myself useful."

Val chuckled. "Well, if you have to hang around."

"Of course. I have your back whenever you need it."

Val's smile evaporated. "Do you really have my back? Because right now, I can't help but feel like we are working at cross-purposes."

"I don't want to be at cross-purposes with you." He moved closer to her, close enough to touch, but he would not be the one to cross that gap first. She'd been clear about her boundaries, and he would respect them. "Listen, while I'm here, I just want to reiterate how sorry I am for hiding the truth about who I am from you."

"You probably wouldn't have gotten very far if I had known."

His heart hammered in his chest at the thought of how his lie had spiraled out of control. "I just wanted to be judged as myself, not as the son of Andreas Wagner. I didn't go about it the right way. But I'm not my father's company."

"What makes you so different? It's your company that's disrupting the community I live in. Why exactly should I trust you?"

"I'm the first to admit, we're botching the community aspect of this project. But—" he inched closer, so close, a breath separated them, but still he didn't touch her "—I don't support people losing their homes. That's not who I am."

Val sighed. "The best thing would be for you guys to go away, but that's not realistic, is it?"

It felt like she'd kicked him. "Do you want me to leave?"

She frowned. "No. I'm the one who invited you. I only meant it'd be great if your company wasn't here. In our backyard." She dropped her eyes, toying with a loose thread on the seam of the seat pillow. Philip waited. Everything between them was so fragile, so uncertain, that if he pushed too hard, things would fall apart.

"Okay," she said at length. "We have a little daylight left. I'll get changed and take you on a tour of *my* neighborhood."

Philip nodded, watching her disappear down a hallway. He rubbed a spot in the middle of his chest where his heart was beating in some uneven rhythm. Val hadn't given Luke the time of day. But she was giving Philip not only a chance to show up, but to also demonstrate that he was worth trusting. He wasn't going to waste that chance.

He perused the titles on her bookshelf, admiring her obvious commitment to collecting every novel in each series. He was examining the dust jacket of a hardback when she returned. She'd tied back her curls in a sleek ponytail, the edges damp, most likely from a quick shower. She wore a pair of dark blue jeans with a rainbow-colored V-neck T-shirt that accentuated the earthy undertone of her skin and matched her kicks. He filed that tidbit in the back of his mind. Colors. Val liked colors and should always be surrounded by the ones that were as vibrant as her personality.

"If we hurry, we can get *piraguas* before Doña Livia closes her cart."

"Shaved ice? That sounds almost like a social encounter."

She pulled a face, which he had to admit, he found irresistibly adorable—nose and lips twisted up as if she'd smelled something decomposing. "I'm just being a good host, that's all."

Chapter Fourteen

They walked along the sidewalk in the waning early evening light. It had been surreal—Philip's appearance on the landing behind Luke, like a spirit she hadn't stopped conjuring since the night she'd walked away from him. She hated the dishonesty, hated what he did and, in the abstract, who he was. But she didn't hate *him*—hate was the farthest thing from her mind when she thought of Philip.

She focused on the task at hand. This was her neighborhood. Her home. He had already shown himself willing to cooperate. This could only help cement his commitment to cooperation. That was the only reason she'd invited him to tour her community with her.

The golden light bathed them in the warmth of possibilities. It was like when her father held her hand. It gave her the strength to believe things would turn out okay.

It was strange to see her own neighborhood from Philip's perspective. There were more than a few eyesores—the abandoned warehouses along the waterfront. Broken concrete overgrown with dandelions and grass that had once been a parking lot. Deformed fences with holes cut out of them or gaps along the edge bent by people trying to get through them instead of over or around them. The dried fountain that looked airbrushed in verdigris at the center of the park that separated East Ward's more well-cared-for blocks from the waterfront.

"The pencil factory you bought also used to make graphite stove polish and fast-color dyes, developed an early form of photolithography and even produced steel," Val said, pointing down the road toward the waterfront, where giant mechanical cranes stretched high over the brick buildings that composed the complex. "Because of that, there was a whole network of businesses and activities that webbed out from there. Those buildings still stand today as apartment buildings and commercial space…" She slid her gaze over to him and caught his expression. "What?"

"Nothing. I didn't know that. But you know, I'd really like to know more about your personal history. The things in the neighborhood that matter to you."

Val gawked at him. "My history? Why?"

Philip kicked at a loose rock, and Val watched it sail into a tuft of green wildflowers blooming out of the pavement. "Because this is your home. It's going to look different to you than it will to me or anyone coming from outside. I can tell you the property value of every single building on this street. And I do know my history. For example, in the 1800s, the Victoria was a respectable hotel that catered to merchants with a bit more money than your average seamen."

Val glanced up at the building again, imagining what life from another time might look like through those now-decrepit windows. "I wasn't aware of that."

Philip nodded, and his gold hair seemed to catch the embers of sunlight that illuminated the sky. "There was a thriving fishing community here in the late 1800s."

"I imagine the bay area was once clean enough to fish," Val said.

"These days, everyone wants to get close to the water, but in those times, the smell of dead fish on the docks was overpowering. People preferred to take lodgings a small distance away rather than stay in the taverns near the water. The Victoria evolved from a hotel to a collection of apartments for rent when the economics of the area changed. The building itself has been here longer than this city has been incorporated."

Val crossed her arms, enjoying this nerdy side of

him. It reminded her of the way he geeked out over *Star Wars*. "I'm impressed. You know your building well."

Philip's face fell. "That's the history you can find on Wikipedia. It's one part of its history, but it isn't the only one, is it? It doesn't tell me anything about the personality of East Ward. Plus—" he bopped her shoulder with his in a companionable way "—knowing you, it's going to be a lot more interesting than knowing the history of the pencil company empire."

"Well," she said, "I am actually way more interesting. But I figured you'd like to see, I don't know, the shops or some distinctive architecture."

"Yes," he said, taking in the walk-ups, storefronts and lots that comprised Val's street. "Architecture is kind of my jam, but I'd enjoy seeing things from your perspective. It is, after all, such a lovely perspective."

"And he's flattering me again," she mumbled loud enough for him to hear her. This neighborhood, this street in particular, had been the stage on which her life had unfolded. There was so much, she didn't know where to start, so she let the geography decide. She pointed at a nondescript building across the street, one not very different from her own.

"My first crush. He used to live there. A Polish boy named Tomasz. We sneaked into his backyard and made out. I didn't realize he'd left a hickey on my neck until my mother saw it when I got home." Val shivered at the memory. "I was grounded for the entire summer. Can you imagine that?"

Philip glared at the building. "He could have asked you permission, instead of condemning you to a summer indoors."

Val considered this reaction and decided she liked him being all indignant on her behalf. "Funny enough," she continued, "that's when I became obsessed with cooking. Cartoons were boring, telenovelas were on repeat because they always went on break over the summer and the only air-conditioning was in the restaurant. It was either work with my parents or go out of my mind with boredom." She glared at him. Was that something he could identify with? "And don't even tell me how you spent your summers because I'll probably barf."

He threw up his hands as if her words had become projectiles that he needed to dodge. "It's probably best if I don't."

"Good. Anyway, I already knew how to cook a few things, but my mom pulled out my grandmother's recipes and she started teaching me everything she knew. I can thank Tomasz for that."

"Good to know he was of some use." Philip was nearly growling and damn, Val didn't realize a man growling could actually be a thing that existed outside of a romance novel. But here was Philip, looking like he might pummel Tomasz if he suddenly appeared. It sent tension twisting through her body, the good kind that made every nerve ending tingle. The kind she was trying her best to ignore.

It didn't help that Philip's long legs were snuggled

tight in a pair of worn jeans that looked soft to the touch. Val squared her shoulders against the temptation to ogle him, from his plaid button up with a clean T-shirt underneath, to his kicks. Even in clothes he might have thrown on as an afterthought, Philip looked good enough to eat.

She really needed to stop imagining what he would taste like. It wasn't helping her concentration one bit.

She gave a quick shake of her head before pointing to a small, fenced-in playground with a decrepit basketball court, the hoops missing the rope for the baskets. "Here is a little park where I used to hang out after school. This bully named Allison used to harass Nati and me."

His mouth—that perfectly shaped mouth, made for kissing—curled into a half smile. "Let me guess. You beat the girl up."

"God, no," Val laughed. "That girl kicked my ass all over the park. I was in third grade and she was this tall fifth grader with freakishly long arms and legs. I went home with a cut lip. But I hit her first, so I'll always have that."

"Wait, so you swung at her even though she was twice your size?"

"She was messing with Nati. I'm the only one who can bully my sister."

Philip laughed. "You don't even have the sense not to start a fight with someone bigger than you."

"As you can see," she said, sweeping her hand in his direction. "I don't have much use for good sense."

"You're not afraid of anything, are you?"

"That's not true. I'm afraid of a lot of things." Of being hurt. Of being betrayed. "But that's not going to stop me from taking on something, even if I have a good chance of losing."

"After what I've learned about you, those might be the truest words you've ever said about yourself."

Val turned away, her blush lighting up her face like the blinking neon sign over the *piraguas* cart toward which they were moving. "Now you're really trying to flatter me."

"I don't need to flatter you about something that is so obvious to anyone paying attention."

Dammit, and now she wanted to kiss him. She hurried down the block, eager to put space between her and the temptation he represented.

They crossed the park to Domingo's Bodega, where Doña Livia had set up her *piraguas* cart for as long as Val could remember. She'd upgraded it over the years until she ran a high-tech, mini ice wagon with a giant, red-and-white umbrella decorated with balloons and streamers, where she scraped ice and mixed rainbow-colored syrup like a wizened magic woman. She even had her own Instagram page, where she posted her more adventurous flavors.

Val hoped the icy sweetness would cool the ever-growing urge to curl around Philip like a stray cat.

The buildings on this side of the park were more elegant. They weren't currently part of the opportunity zone Philip's company was interested in developing. The brownstones had carefully tended flower boxes that actually held flowers, now that the weather was reasonable. Ivy snaked up the side of buildings with worn but not pockmarked brick. It was one of Val's favorite places, and she was grateful Philip's company had no plans for now.

Not Philip's company. Wagner Developments. She was trying her best to decouple the man and the business in her mind.

"Valeria." Doña Livia came around from behind her cart and they exchanged a kiss on the cheek, the woman's gray-streaked black hair tickling Val's skin. Despite the warm weather, her hands and cheeks were chilly from working with ice all day long.

Doña Livia offered her hand to Philip, making the weakest effort to be discreet as she studied him from crown to foot. Val exchanged a look with him over the older woman's head, biting back a smirk at how nosy she was.

When Doña Livia was satisfied with her scrutiny, she turned her attention to Val. "I saw your father, taking his usual walk. *Lo veo bien, sabes.*"

Everyone who knew her father before his wife's death always made a point of commenting on how good he looked, even though it had been more than a decade since she'd passed. As if by asking, they could keep him from being anything but in good health.

"He's good, thank God."

"*Me allegro*. So, what would you like?"

Every flavor of *piragua* came to mind before she could shape the names in Spanish—or English. She loved *guanabana* and *parcha*, but also strawberry and coconut, and sometimes multiple syrups combined. But tonight, Philip was here and it felt celebratory, despite her best efforts to restrain her excitement. It called for something decadent.

"Crema, por favor."

Doña Livia got to work scraping and shaping the cone, the sound of metal against ice a soothing and familiar one from the days when Val was a child, jumping up and down with a quarter in hand, impatient for her own cone. After Doña Livia handed Val her *piragua*, she asked Philip for his preference.

"I'll have what she's having."

Doña Livia nodded in approval, as if she could determine the quality of Philip's character from his choice in *piragua* flavors. She handed him his cone and watched as he took a small bite of ice, hissing at the cold. His lips puckered, which put Val in the mind of licking warmth back into them.

"This is good. I usually associate *piraguas* with fruit syrup," he said.

Doña Livia puffed herself out with pride. "Si, but these are *piragua de crema*—more ice cream than ice."

Val thanked Doña Livia. When Val paid—and she

insisted on paying because that dinner at the French restaurant would bug her forever—they walked along the street to an ivy-covered building with an engraved brass plaque fixed next to the door.

"This building belonged to the son of a Puerto Rican poet, who was forced to leave the island in the seventies because he belonged to the Independence movement. His daughter still runs a book club for the older ladies in the neighborhood."

"A neighborhood book club? Does she use the library or does she hold the meetings here?" Philip asked, reading the inscription on the building out loud—Rubén Mounier, 1944–2018.

"No, she does it here, in her father's old salon. I've been meaning to come but I never have the time. The young women read modern books. But the *señoras*, they want their old-school romances and you won't pry those out of their wrinkled little hands."

"Val," Philip interjected, "was there some kind of artist community here in the past?"

Pride in East Ward bubbled up in her. "Yes. Besides everything else…" She let the emphasis linger on that the word *else*, which did not escape his notice by the small nod he gave. "It's a sister city to a small town outside Ponce."

"Ponce, isn't that where the Museo de Arte is located?"

"It is," Val said, impressed by his knowledge. "Have you been there?"

"I visited once. We had a commercial project outside San Juan. I took a few days of vacation to explore the island."

"Alone?" Val felt her eyes grow so wide, her face ached. She had no business asking him that, not if this was intended to be just an informational walk.

Philip's smirk was knowing enough to trigger a burning sensation in her chest. She turned away before he caught her embarrassment. "You know what? I don't really want to know."

His long stride brought him to her side again. "It's nothing sordid. I went with a friend who happened to work for the company competing against us for the project."

"Touring with the enemy. Seems to be a theme with you," she retorted. His laugh was crystalline and it lit up…everything. She was so annoyed with herself for being so damned taken by him. They weren't friends. "We have one last stop."

She lapsed into silence as they walked, finishing the last of their *piraguas*. When they were done, they tossed their soggy paper cones in a trash can.

Philip reached a hand out to stop her. "Are you okay?"

That pulled her up short. "Why wouldn't I be? This way." She led him up the block, wrestling with her reaction to him. She had absolutely no reason to feel anything at all about his personal life or decisions. So it was a colleague and not something more romantic. That was not her business either way. It wasn't like she owned the island. He was free to go wherever he wanted with whomever he wanted. The fact that it bothered the hell out of her was completely irrelevant to anything.

They arrived at a nondescript corner, cars drifting by on a cross street toward the busier boulevard up ahead. Old lovers and fantastic plans about the future were relegated to a dark corner of her mind, taken over by other, more momentous memories.

"And here…" She stopped, raising a hand to caress the traffic post, a mechanical beeping indicating that it was safe to cross. "Here is where my mother died."

"Here?" Philip looked around. There was nothing to see. Years flowed between where she stood now and where she had been back then. Time was like a giant street sweeper, collecting the wreckage of broken lives and erasing them, except in the memory of the people who lived them. Val's memory. And Val never forgot anything.

Val clutched the rosary that always hung around her neck. "I was walking right next to her. She stepped off the curb to cross, and a motorcycle going too fast clipped her. She fell and hit her head." She stared at the asphalt, the scene unfolding before her eyes. "She got up, spoke to me and Doña Livia, who helped me take her back to the restaurant. We got her to the hospital but maybe we were too slow, or maybe she wasn't as strong as I thought she was, I don't know. She lost consciousness and never woke up again."

Philip grew pale in the waning light. He rubbed

his face, scraping at the five o'clock shadow that was emerging along his jaw.

"How do you do it?" he whispered. "How can you walk by this place every day and not break?"

She didn't answer. Maybe she didn't pull it off as well as she thought she did.

"I could never…" Philip said, but the words died on his lips.

"I know it's not an anecdote you can bring back to your company or investors or whoever. This stop was only for you, to help you understand me a little." She had to crane to look up at him and realized that throughout their entire walk, she had forgotten how very tall he was, or maybe she couldn't help but feel very small, especially in this spot, sharing this memory. She tore her gaze away, focusing on the ground instead.

"The place is a little grungy." She kicked at a soft drink cup that hadn't quite made it into the trash. "Could definitely use a cleanup. But there is a community here worth preserving. This isn't some plastic toy you buy at the store, use until it gets old and throw away for a new one."

Philip at least had the decency to look miserable. "I offered you my cooperation."

"But you have to mean it, not just for publicity or to save face. These things have a domino effect. First, it was the waterfront, then the Victoria. Soon it will be the building with Navarro's inside. And that I can't allow." She remembered Felicia's admonishment to not talk to him about her intentions to buy the building. There was no reason to give him that advantage. "My family put too much into that restaurant. I'm all for improving the neighborhood but not the way you're going about it."

Philip reached out, curling a lock of her hair around his finger. The action knocked her off her center. He hadn't touched her since their failed date, and she'd spent far too many nights trying not to remember how it felt to have his hands on her. This walk would already set her back, sending her into an endless obsession over every word they'd exchanged, every gesture he made. There weren't enough surfaces left in her building to clean for her to purge her feelings.

"If it's not us, it'll be someone else. You understand that, don't you? There's just not enough private capital here to do what companies like ours do on a large scale."

"I know things change, but do we always have to be the ones left behind?"

He made to speak but dropped his hand instead. She was grateful, because having him this close, with night just a half sunset away and crickets already chirping, made her wish she could stop thinking altogether and finish what they'd started on the walkway. She had to focus on what mattered. He had no answer to her question. No one did, unless they were planning to remake the world anew, and that was not in either of their power.

They resumed their walk, completing a circuit that brought them back to her building. Philip stopped in front of the Victoria. Val always passed this building, but it was as if she was seeing it for the first time. Metal scaffolds hung off the front and side of the building like metal insects, clinging to the chipped brick facade. It looked old and tired, like many of the buildings on this street.

And Val's building next door, like a domino, waiting to fall.

She wouldn't let it. Everything had been set in motion, pending approval of their mortgage, which they'd hear back about soon. She wasn't going to let them take everything away from her. Philip scanned the building, making his own evaluations. He didn't need to know her plans. She couldn't risk having anyone derail them.

They returned to Navarro's. The windows were dark, but the apartments above were illuminated. Her family was up there. The Gutierrezes. The other tenants who comprised the ad hoc group of people who called this place home. Their intimate space. Borrowed space, if things didn't go well.

"I should probably get going," Philip said, but with the urgency of someone who had nowhere to go. His hands buried deep in his pocket made him look younger, far less confident than the persona he normally projected. Val was tempted to invite him up for coffee. But they'd done what they set out to do, and she'd insisted that this not be a social visit.

If she didn't show some fortitude, he might think she'd give in easily to other, more serious things. She couldn't afford that kind of vulnerability.

It was hard being a responsible, functioning adult, complete with boundaries and limitations. Especially when the more impulsive side of her wanted to throw off that pesky maturity and do the exact opposite of enforcing boundaries.

"Good night," she said, stumbling over her words. "And thank you."

Despite his height, he still managed to look at her from under his lashes, longer and more golden than anyone had any business possessing. He nodded, and pulled the car key fob from his pocket, slowly, as if waiting for her to change my mind.

"It's always a good night, with you." He turned to get into his car but Val lunged forward, stopping just short of the passenger door. It had been impulsive and foolish and now she scrambled to come up with something to say.

"You'll reach out to us about that meeting, right?"

Philip gave her a wry smile and Val hated, absolutely hated, how transparent she was. "As soon as I get my team together."

Val swung her arms, snapping her fingers, unsure what else to say or do. The realization that she was stalling his departure forced her to take a step back. "Right. Okay."

"We'll talk." He hesitated, as if he had more to

say, before settling into the car and putting it in motion.

She didn't want to be one of those people who stared as others drove off, but that was exactly who she was as Philip started his car, put it in gear and pulled away. She watched until his taillights dimmed to nothing in the dark.

Chapter Fifteen

Philip arranged a meeting with Morales and representatives of East Ward Fair Housing Coalition before the following week was out. The community liaison he'd asked Leighton to appoint was in place, but Philip decided to stay on and oversee negotiations. He wanted to make sure things were done right. For the sake of the company, the community. For Val.

He had no occasion to communicate with Val between her personal tour of her neighborhood and the meeting. When the day arrived, he watched the conference room door attentively, beyond excited to see her again. She wasn't the only reason he organized the meeting, but she was the biggest incentive.

She arrived dressed in a white, button-down business shirt that highlighted the flawless olive tone of her skin and sensible slacks that hinted at her curves. She'd tied her hair back into a ponytail that made her look incredibly young. When she caught sight of him, her smile was quick and spontaneous before she appeared to remember herself and toned it down. But it had been enough to buoy his mood.

They got down to work. While Morales led the meeting, Val impressed him with how deeply informed she was on minutiae about which most people outside of real estate and development didn't bother. The meeting about the Victoria was part of a larger effort to codify protections into laws that future developers would have to work with, so Philip took great care with the details. They also scheduled a follow-up meeting to formalize a proposed Community Benefits Agreement that Andreas Wagner would approve.

"This was a good session," Morales said by way of conclusion. "It far exceeded our expectations."

"It will save everyone time and energy in the future. We'll meet again after I've discussed the draft with my father."

Morales shook Philip's hand. "Excuse me if I run out of here," she said, addressing Val, as well. "I have another meeting to get to."

"Thank you," Val said, giving Morales a quick hug before the lawyer took her things and raced as politely as she could from the room. Everyone else had filed out, leaving Philip alone with Val. She shuffled her already-sorted papers while he tapped his pen against his notepad. Even with everyone gone from the room, and the skyline stretching out endlessly beyond the wall of windows, Philip felt claustrophobic.

"I feel really positive about this," Val said. "Thank you."

"It was a group effort." The last thing he wanted was her gratitude for something he felt was the minimum concession for a company to make.

"No one person can do everything alone." She held her leather portfolio against her chest, and he was back on her street again, unable to say goodbye to her.

"It's almost twelve. I don't know what your afternoon looks like, but there's a deli up the block that makes excellent sandwiches and they don't make you wait too long."

Val glanced out the window, the hesitation evident in the pensive way she stared at the buildings before turning her attention back to him. "It's a nice day for a walk."

"Especially after being cooped up in here. Come on. My treat. You can leave your things in my office and we'll get them later."

Val handed him her portfolio. "There better be prices on the menu or I'm walking out."

Philip's laugh came from a deep place in his chest, a dam of anxiety and longing bursting free. He hadn't felt this good in days. Not since the last time he'd been with her.

"There are prices everywhere. It was my first criterion for suggesting it."

Val broke out in a smile. "I haven't had a good pastrami sandwich in ages, even if I usually end up wearing half of it."

Philip rounded the conference room table to hold the door open for her, hoping he didn't look too ridiculous in his giddiness. "We can arrange for a bib if we have to."

They ended up not needing a bib. But it really was too nice a day to sit inside the cramped deli. They took their sandwiches and drinks and made their way down to the waterfront, where they found a free bench in the park overlooking the river. Val felt like a kid playing hooky from school—lunch hour was rush hour in her restaurant, and she was always there for it. Her usual diffidence toward Philip had calmed down after working with him all morning. She always knew he was intelligent and something about him exuded competence. But his command of details was impressive. As a business owner, she could respect that.

She'd taken a chance accepting his lunch invitation but had been generously rewarded by a still-steaming pastrami sandwich, sour-cream-and-chives-flavored chips and an enormous side of Philip Wagner, taking up half the bench with his corporate fineness.

Happy Tuesday to me.

Thankfully, she had the presence of mind to buy an extra-large bottle of water, because the thirst was real out here.

"So which one of these high-rises do you live in?" Val asked between bites, spicy mustard stinging her lips.

"What makes you think I live in a high-rise?"

"I don't know." She tapped primly at her lips with a paper napkin. "Your company does massive development projects, so you probably have your pick of apartment units. You're a single workaholic, so you probably don't want to waste time commuting and I don't see you riding the A train with the rest of us plebeians." She caught his side-eye, which made her laugh harder. "So you have to live close by."

"Ah, now you see, that's where your preconceptions cause you to miscalculate. As a matter of fact, I don't live in a high-rise. I live in a renovated warehouse."

"Top floor?"

"Okay, yes," he conceded. "Fair point. But—" he pulled out his wallet and slid the telltale MetroCard from its sleeve "—I like it there because it's one stop to my work and I like the space."

"It wasn't a judgment or anything. I was just curious. But I bet you have a housekeeper."

"I do happen to have someone who comes in once a week to clean up the place, but that's only because I work a lot and I'd rather use my limited free time for other things."

Val shifted on the bench so she was facing him. They were so different, she couldn't help being curious about the way he lived. "What do you like to do with your free time?"

"Like you, I enjoy running."

"How…? Oh, you saw the track trophies." She smiled at how observant he was. "I've run the entire waterfront from my house to Exchange Place."

"You're better than me," he laughed.

"What else?"

"I also enjoy watching movies in movie theaters. I've seen every single *Star Wars* movie on the big screen, and trust me, it makes a difference."

"Damned straight," Val said, offering him a fist bump, which he obliged.

"And I take my Italian girl out for pleasure drives on the weekends."

"Oh, that sounds nice. I can't do that. My jalopy doesn't approve of aimless driving."

Philip turned to her; she saw how a part of his sandwich was still wrapped in the wax paper. "If your jalopy doesn't get too offended, I could offer to take you for a drive in my car this weekend."

Val took a deep breath. He made it all sound so easy. They could easily be two coworkers, having lunch on a park bench, making plans for the weekend. She didn't mistrust him completely—after the whole withholding his identity situation, he'd been honest with her and come through on the proposed agreement.

But it wasn't a done deal yet. And she was terrified of any missteps that might jeopardize that.

"Maybe, after everything is signed and done with, we can celebrate together."

Philip frowned. "You don't trust me, do you?"

Val's appetite suddenly shriveled up. Which was a shame—the sandwich was one of the best she'd had. "It's not a question of trust. Not…completely. It's more about propriety, you know? It's not right to mix things up when we don't know how it all will end."

"I hear what you're saying," he answered, his eyes losing focus as he got lost in his thoughts. "But one thing doesn't have to depend on the other. I wouldn't jeopardize our work because of things that happen, or don't happen, between us."

She wanted to believe that. But people had a tendency to have more faith in their own goodness than sometimes was merited. Ethics were relative and it was easy to believe a version of the truth that suited the situation. She'd learned that lesson the hard way, and she wasn't sure she wanted to risk a situation like that again.

"I'll think about it," she said finally.

Philip sighed but nodded. "Fair enough. Are you going to finish your chips?"

Val narrowed her eyes at him, but truthfully, she was full and she appreciated the way he was trying to lighten the mood. Rejection was a bitch, even if it had nothing to do with how much she liked him. "You're a scavenger."

"I am. Can't stand to waste food."

Val's eyes went wide. "You sound just like Mom. She was always going on about waste. Don't leave the lights on. Don't eat with your eyes. Don't—"

"Wait, don't eat with your eyes?" He shook his head, his expression adorably confused. "What does that mean?"

"It's a saying. It just means don't serve yourself more food than you can eat."

"That…makes absolutely no sense."

Val frowned. "It actually does sound better in Spanish." She chuckled to herself. "I'm so used to our sayings, I don't bother to think them through very deeply."

Philip leaned against the bench. At some point, he'd stretched his arm so it rested behind her back. Her awareness of it brought a prickly heat to her skin, which became worse when he brought his hand up to tuck a curl that had come lose behind her ear. "It's sweet. I like your sayings."

She looked away before he could trap her with his touch. He was easy to be with, but there was that thing between them that always found a way to bubble up and overrun their moments. She wished she had control over this craving that tethered her to him. Her breathing grew uneven and she fiddled with the wrapper of her sandwich. She ventured a glance at him.

"I should get back to the restaurant. It's usually crazy busy at this time."

A furrow appeared between Philip's eyes, but it disappeared when he chased it away with a smile. "Let's get you back then."

Their return walk was quiet. People still milled about in the fine weather, and Val envied their apparent carefree pleasure. Whereas she ached and wanted and didn't dare put a name to what she wanted.

"It was nice, Val," he said, the words sounding like he was talking about more than just a nice lunch. It was always more than just nice with him.

"You'll keep us posted on your father's feedback?" She felt like a broken record, asking about one thing when she really wanted to know something else. But she didn't dare tell Philip how much she wanted to hear from him just because, so the proposal was as much neutral territory as she could hope for.

"You can depend on it," he answered. Val took the portfolio from his outstretched hand and clutched it to her chest like a shield. Who or what she was shielding, she didn't interrogate too deeply, but it was high time she got out of there before her resolve failed her completely.

"We'll talk," she said. "Thanks. For lunch."

"Anytime." His hands were deep in his pockets again and for an insane moment, she wanted to drop the portfolio and throw her arms around him. That's when she knew it was time for her to go.

Chapter Sixteen

When Val left, Philip made his way to his office. His concentration was shot again but a tennis match wasn't going to solve the problem this time.

Val still didn't trust him, which bothered him more than he wanted to admit. They'd done good work today, partly because their teams had been able to compromise with the expectation that they were all acting in good faith. The belief that what they were doing was good and fair and right. The scope of the meeting had extended beyond just the tenants of the Victoria and the waterfront, but also moved into questions of labor and unions, which would require a follow-up meeting to resolve. It had been a very good day.

But Val's trust issues were more personal, and Philip had contributed to those issues by being dishonest in the beginning. It was a rocky foundation for any relationship, and he wished he knew a workaround for that.

First things first. He had to figure out a way to get his father on board with the draft proposal. He asked his mother to help him by reserving dinner at one of his father's favorite restaurants. Getting him out of the office could only help Philip's cause.

That's how, a few nights later, the three of them found themselves seated in Pirandello's, an exclusive restaurant in downtown Hoboken, with his father wrinkling his nose, not at the menu, but at the proposal Philip had given him earlier in the afternoon.

"When you said you would work with the community representatives, it was not with the intention of giving away the store," Andreas grumbled, passing the file with his notes to Philip.

"Now, Andreas." Philip's mother's voice still held a sweet lilt that reflected her wealthy Kentucky equestrian roots. She gave Philip a warm, indulgent smile, placing her hand over his. "Philip always does such excellent work. I'm sure if he's made a decision, he's done so with good reason."

Philip gave her hand a grateful squeeze. She'd always been his biggest champion, even when he and his father were at odds. She had faith in his judgment and he felt like every success was a reward for her belief in him. Unlike his father, who sometimes gave or withheld his affections based on Philip's performance, his mother was Team Philip, no matter what he did.

"I'm not questioning his judgment, Grace," his father retorted, though with less antagonism than before. Mom would have never put up with that. "But twenty percent of capacity reserved for current tenants and an additional twenty percent for moderate income units? It's not what we sold to investors."

"Then they'll pull out and pay the penalties to do so," Philip answered. "There are other ways to get funding."

"Oh, because money falls like manna from the sky?" Andreas sputtered.

"I meant selling more public bonds. The area is in demand and the city is willing. Money won't be the issue."

"Hmm, apple doesn't fall far from the tree, it would seem." Grace chuckled, taking a sip of water, her long fingers lightly wrapped around her glass, slick with condensation. Lifting his own drink to his lips, Philip thought of Val and her own strong hands that bore burn scars, hands he could kiss from the calloused tip to her slim wrist.

Andreas's ears grew pink at the tips, and his jaw worked as if he were grinding stones. The waiter appeared with their menus, and Grace accepted them, thanking him with her usual delicacy.

"I won't be bested by my own son," Andreas said when the waiter left them alone again.

Philip frowned. He didn't like it when his father slipped into zero-sum-game mode. "This isn't about besting anyone. It's my company, too. We're flipping properties that already have occupants living in them. I never thought we were in the business of throwing people out on the street."

"No one is being thrown out on the street," Andreas retorted. "We provide ample warning and invite tenants to remain if they're able to pay for the modest increases in rent."

"'Modest increases,' he says. Okay, Dad." Philip resisted rolling his eyes. He wasn't going to get into an argument with his father in public. "I suggest you double check those figures. The increases have been anything but modest."

Andreas deflated, appearing more like the father he knew in private, not the ruthless corporate raider who wouldn't hesitate to mow someone down if it meant reaching his objective. "I'll go back and look. But regardless of what I decide, acquisitions will proceed as planned, even if we're forced to make accommodations."

Grace crossed her arms, considering her husband. "Is that the sound of a compromise being made? I never thought I'd see the day."

It was Philip's turn to smile. "Miracles happen."

Andreas gave Grace a sidelong glance and Philip caught the slippage of his father's armor. He was a hard-ass, but his mother wasn't afraid to call him out when she needed to. She'd long ago turned her energies to building The Wagner Foundation and now mostly focused on the charitable organization. But Philip had the suspicion that, had she chosen otherwise, she would have given his father a run for his business money.

Andreas drummed his fingers on the table as they ordered. He'd gone impassive again, except for the nervous tapping. "Something else?" Philip asked.

"One of our potential properties has gone under contract for sale."

"Congratulations?"

Andreas stopped his tapping. "No, it's not being sold to us. I wouldn't be surprised if the purchase itself were an act of protest against our interest in the property."

Of course, his father would take it personally. "People are free to buy and sell as they like."

"Not if I have a say," Andreas retorted.

Philip felt his pique rising. "You don't control everything."

"Enough talk of your business," Grace interjected, filling everyone's glass of wine. "Let's talk about mine."

Philip backed down, and even Andreas visibly relaxed. "Charity is not business."

"I beg to differ, darling," Grace said, unperturbed by his comment. "I'm holding a fundraiser next weekend and I'd love it if you came, Philip. Étienne will be there."

"Are you two working on another project to-gether?" Philip asked.

Grace's eyes, the very same deep shade of blue as Philip's, twinkled but she simply shrugged in response.

"What are you two plotting?" Andreas asked, also catching Grace's mood.

Grace practically danced in her chair. "Well, if you insist. We're thinking about auctioning off a limited edition bound photography series. It's a huge draw because the photography is his."

"Nothing like a nice family photo series by Étienne Galois," Andreas said, refilling his wine-glass.

Grace laughed. "Oh, no, love, we don't want this to be family photographs. We're thinking more like the style of his last series."

Étienne was riding the wave of a successful series celebrating human sexuality. His photographs were posted all over social media, and his exhibit had been written up in all the major fashion magazines.

Philip leaned back, nodding with admiration. "That's really progressive for your charity."

"Oh, darling." She waved her hand—and his words—away. "We keep up with the times. Plus, those photographs are absolutely stunning."

The tone of her voice as she described the photos made Philip uneasy. Andreas was again quick to react. "Grace! Are you ogling young models?"

"No, but that exhibit is quite possibly the sexiest thing I've ever seen. That's why it's so popular."

The expression on his father's face was almost worth Philp's discomfort at the knowledge that his mother showed any kind of interest in sex. "Why on Earth would you admire those models when have me?"

"Okay," Philip said, shooting to his feet. Maybe the look on his father's face was not worth it after all. "Time for a bathroom break."

"Oh, dear, who would have thought you were such a modest thing?" Grace teased as Philip walked away, her voice dropping to a low whisper in response to some comment his father made.

But Philip's mind was whirling. His father was hesitant about the proposal. That he didn't reject it outright was a good sign, but he might need a nudge in the right direction. The fundraiser would be a perfect opportunity to do this. He'd bring Val, if she accepted, and introduce them to each other. Right now, the work in East Ward was just buildings and plans, but if Andreas met Val, he would be putting a face on the work they were doing. It was hard to run roughshod over someone when the personal stakes were revealed. Val's tour of her neighborhood had taught him that.

It would also be a way to earn Val's trust, once and for all. She was still holding herself back from him despite an obvious attraction, as if she were ready at every turn to defend herself. He acknowledged his own responsibility in that. But some of it came from her past, and some days, he just wanted to reach back into her history and punch the fool who'd put those fears in her.

Besides, his mother planned some of the best parties. Étienne would be there, most likely with Malena, which would help Val feel more at ease. Unlike his father's fondness for zero-sum games, Philip preferred everyone to win. And he'd get to spend an evening with Val, and that was possibly the best part of all.

Chapter Seventeen

Val leaned against the counter with hot tea in hand, relieved that the last customer had finally left. She had another hour to go before closing but she'd hoped to start cleanup early and maybe get in a run. It had been a mild day, the ever-lengthening hours sliding into a warm if breezy evening. It would free her mind from work, awaiting approval for the mortgage on their building, and the proposed changes negotiated between the EWFHC and Wagner Developments.

She wondered, as she often did, what Philip might do on a night like this. She quickly punted the thought out of her brain.

Nati calling Val from the kitchen snapped her out of her thoughts.

"Are you here?" Nati asked.

"Where else?" Val answered, taking another sip of tea. When Nati appeared, she wasn't in her scrubs, but freshly washed and cheerfully radiant despite a twelve-hour shift. Val would kill for a scrub down with her loofah about now. It might clear her thinking and keep her mind from flying to the same place— or person—every single damned time.

"I'm here now, *hermana*," Nati sang, giving Val a sloppy kiss on the cheek. "Want some help with cleanup?"

Val's mood instantly lifted. "Yeah! Want to have dinner first?"

"Oh, I ate already. I'm too wired to sleep so I figured I'd be useful. Where is everybody?" Nati answered, tying an apron behind her back.

Nati had an uncanny ability to know when Val needed the most help. In fact, she'd lucked out with her siblings. Neither had ever said no when she needed backup in the restaurant. "Papi had an appointment. Everyone else either called in or had to go home. Today was a mess."

"Well, didn't I show up in time?" Nati chirped, getting to work right away on clearing off the last of the tables.

Val's phone vibrated. She took another sip of tea and pulled it out of her pocket.

"Oh," she mumbled.

"What is it?" Nati said, pulling the phone over to look at the text.

"It's Philip. You know, Philip Wagner. Says he wants to stop by and see me," Val said, glancing at herself in the mirror above the espresso maker.

Nati's easy smile evaporated as she leaned in close to her sister, dropping her voice to a whisper. "I thought he was public enemy number one? He's making house calls?"

Val grimaced. She hadn't told Nati about giving him a tour of the neighborhood. It had been strangely personal, and she hadn't wanted to submit it to the collective scrutiny of her family. But Nati was fully aware of the work EWFHC was doing with Philip and his people.

"Maybe it has to do with our last meeting," Val said, rubbing her rosary between her thumb and forefinger.

"Didn't you say it went well?" Nati handed the phone back to Val.

"It did. So I'm not sure what he wants to talk about. What if it's bad news?"

Nati pointed at Val's phone. "Ask him."

Val nodded and tapped out her message.

Is it anything I have to worry about?

His answer was almost instantaneous. She really hoped he wasn't driving.

Nothing bad. Promise. Just a proposition Maybe we can discuss over dinner?

Dinner? That was even more nerve-racking. "No bad news," she said. "But he said he could tell me over dinner."

Nati tapped her chin, thinking. "Maybe ask him to stay for dinner instead of going somewhere else. You know—keep your enemies close and well-fed."

Val tilted her head, considering her sister. "Did you read that in one of your manuals, Dr. Machiavelli?"

Nati gave Val a glare before shaking her head. "No. Everybody knows men dig food."

"I think the whole species digs food, *hermanita*."

Val typed out a message to Philip with Nati's laughter ringing in the background. Dinner in her restaurant wasn't a half-bad idea. It would give her a sense of control, at least until she found out what he wanted from her.

Last customer just left. How about we have dinner here?

Once again, Philip's response was immediate, and their exchange became as lively as always.

I don't want to trouble you. Just wanted to ask you about something.

No trouble. It's not like I'm cooking. It's already prepared.

Okay. OMW

Don't you want to know what's on the menu?

I'll eat anything.

Except goat.

Except goat :)

Val tucked her phone in her back pocket. "We'll have dinner here."

Nati chuckled. "You better get it ready, because I think he's the one parking his car out front."

"What?" Val rushed to the front door, peering through the letters glued onto the windows of the restaurant.

"Nobody in this neighborhood owns an Alfa Romeo." Nati gazed out the window, as well. "He's not playing around, is he? The man literally texted from outside your door," Nati chortled before peering more closely at him.

Val ignored her, panic clawing up her chest. "He's here. I need lipstick," Val said as she darted past her.

"Why do you need lipstick? Val!" Nati called, following her to the bathroom in her father's office.

"Just because it's a business thing doesn't mean I have to look washed out." Val half crawled under the sink, rummaging through the bottles and pouches stuffed inside.

Nati shot a hand past her and grabbed a bulging

gold lamé case. She pulled out a tube and handed it to Val.

"Here. Courtesy of Fenty Beauty. It's the good stuff."

Val applied the lip gloss and smoothed down her hair before turning toward her sister. "Well?"

"Supermodel. Now go. He just walked in."

"He's here. Okay." Val took a long, deep breath, clutching her rosary as she numbered off what was available. "*Pernil*. Rice. Beans, *maduros, ensalada…*"

"I think he broke your brain," Nati said between chuckles.

Val shook herself. "No, no, I'm good. Right as rain." She smoothed out her apron and walked toward the front. She had no reason to act like she'd never seen a man before.

The tinkling bell gave away his arrival. Val popped her head around the wall of the kitchen.

Philip wore a dark gray-blue suit vest, sleeves rolled up to his elbow to reveal perfectly defined forearms, top buttons of his dress shirt undone. She imagined him tearing his jacket and tie off as he left his office, reserving the careful work of rolling up his sleeves and unbuttoning the top two buttons for when he was relaxed in the driver's seat. He'd finish undressing when he got home, discarded shirt and undone pants pooled at his feet.

The visual. She had to get that visual out of her head.

She was self-conscious about her worn jeans and

faded red T-shirt beneath her stained apron. She had readjusted the bandanna that held her hair back, hoping the festive color would brighten her work-worn appearance.

"Someone told me dinner was to die for," he said by way of greeting.

"Don't die," she said with a shaky laugh. "It'd be bad for business."

Philip's eyes flicked over her before scanning the restaurant. "It looks even cozier during the day." His gaze lingered on the large mural at the far end of the restaurant. "I liked that painting the first time I saw it."

"It's Arecibo, the town my father is from."

"It's exceptional," Philip said as he studied it.

"This building has quite a few murals. They were painted back when East Ward was an artist community. Maybe I'll show you one day."

Wait.

No.

She clamped down on her tongue before she said any other idiotic things.

He turned back to her, the entire force of his gaze leaving her wanting for oxygen. "I'd like that very much."

"Let's take this table here," she said quickly, leading him toward her preferred booth. A flourishing tree grew outside the window, bark mottled by pollution and the carvings of couple's names. It was majestic but its roots were distorting the concrete around it. She expected the city to come out and take care of it at some point, but until then, she enjoyed it while watching people walk along the sidewalk, the thick leaves shading them from the worst of the sun.

"I don't want to give you more work. We can always go somewhere else."

"It's really no prob—" The clatter of pots erupting from the kitchen cut across Val's words. She hurried toward the swinging doors. "Nati? Are you okay?"

"Sorry, they slipped out of my hand," Nati answered with a decidedly unapologetic tone. She glanced past Val to where Philip sat watching them. Nati lowered her voice to a whisper. "I didn't mean to interrupt you guys."

Val rolled her eyes. "Yeah, okay. Come meet him."

She led her extra-nosy sister to the table. Philip stood upon their approach like a perfect gentleman.

"You must be Philip," Nati said, not bothering to wait for Val.

"Nati. Val talks about you all the time."

"Nothing good, I hope."

Philip appeared caught off guard by her comment, but he recovered quickly. "Not one good thing, now that I think of it."

Nati raised an eyebrow before a laugh burst out of her. "Good to know my reputation precedes me."

Val watched as Philip gave Nati a smile that bedazzled them both before taking her hand. "Nice to meet you."

Nati stood with her mouth gaping open. Val almost pitied her. "Since Philip and I are going to have dinner, I'll take care of cleanup."

Nati managed to tear her gaze away from Philip long enough to answer her sister. "I already said I'd do it. You guys take as much time as you need."

No way. Nati thought she was going to weasel her way into hanging around, but it wasn't happening. "You really don't have to. I know you have things to do," Val said, her eyes boring into her sister's, sending her a message she was clearly intent on ignoring.

"No I don't. Anyway, I've done cleanup a million times. I can handle it. Want me to help you get your plates ready?"

She was going to throttle her in the kitchen. "Yeah, sure, why not?" Val answered. She turned her attention to Philip, who was still standing, watching them with a humorous expression. "One special coming right up."

"Sounds perfect," he answered. Nati gave Philip moon eyes once more before turning and following Val to the back.

"Not a word," Val snapped when Nati began to speak.

"You did not tell me that the bad corporate man was so cute," Nati said, talking over her.

"He's not entirely bad." Val murmured, then silently cursed herself.

"But he's still a Wagner so you have to be careful. Hey, you don't think he's here because he wants to talk you out of buying the building?"

"Shh," Val snapped. "He doesn't know I put in an offer."

"Good to know you don't trust him, either." Nati's words left her hollow, but they were also the truth. "Well, I'm sticking around, just in case."

"Nati!" Val objected, but Nati used her selective hearing to ignore her and busied herself arranging plates on the tray. Val's shoulders slumped. "Fine. Just don't hover."

"I'm not going to hover. I'm not weird."

"So you say," Val retorted. "Help me carry the trays?"

"Okay. But before you do that…" Nati stepped behind her, undoing the knot and pulling off both the bandanna and the apron. "These are not high-fashion accessories." She finger-combed Val's hair until she was satisfied. "Now you look like an off-duty restaurant worker."

"*Tonta,*" Val snapped, which made Nati laugh harder and brought a smile to Val's face. Nati's chortles followed Val to where Philip sat studying the restaurant as if he hadn't spent the night with her there.

Val tried to see Navarro's through his eyes. What she saw tugged at her heart—the kitchen where she used to follow her mother around as a child, learning to cook. Tables where she'd done her homework, illuminated by sunlight. This was her home, an extension of who she was, and she was sharing it with him.

"Dinner is served," Val said, ignoring her sister's grin as they set down the trays. When Philip looked at her, the hair along the nape of her neck stood at attention. She struggled with the equally powerful impulses to both run away from him and crawl into his lap, each reaction more disconcerting than the other.

Nati helped Val arrange the plates before tucking the serving trays under her arm. "If you kids need anything else, just wave at me."

"Thanks, Nati."

"Oh, please, you never take a break." She turned toward Philip, jabbing a thumb in Val's direction. "It's a good thing you showed up or she'd be running till midnight."

"She strikes me as pretty driven."

Nati waved her hands at Val. "If Val didn't exist, someone would have had to invent her."

She wandered off, leaving Philip with his brow furrowed. "Your sister is nice but she speaks in riddles, too."

"Oh." Val laughed. "She just translated a Spanish saying. I think what she means to say is that I'm unique, though she doesn't always mean it as a compliment."

He leaned forward so that only she could hear him. "I agree with her. And I mean that entirely as a compliment."

Her heart unstuck itself from her chest and ended up somewhere in her throat. She took too much time unfolding the napkin Nati had added to the tray and placing it over her lap.

He took a bite of the pork and let out a low moan.

Val froze as the sound exploded through her body. This had been a terrible idea. Not only did she have to wait to find out what he wanted, but he was inadvertently edging her with nothing more than the sound of his pleasure. She clenched her legs shut, releasing a shuddering breath, praying he wouldn't notice. It was excruciating to sit opposite him and not climb across the table, scattering plates and cups to do filthy things to his mouth.

"This is excellent," he said when he finished chewing.

"You think?" Val squeaked before clearing her throat. "You should eat it with the rice and beans. Some people mix it with the cassava." She pointed at the white root on his plate, smothered in onions. "Or you can dip the meat in the *mojo*."

"Garlic?"

Val handed him one of the small bowls with shaky hands. "Not just garlic. There's olive oil, cilantro, lemon and salt, as well."

Philip looked at his dish. "I'll try it your way." He followed her suggestion, dipping his pork in the *mojo*, nodding his approval all the while. Satisfaction spread, warm and syrupy through her veins, an improvement over her animal lust.

Val rarely got to play the customer in her own restaurant. She savored the flavors that reminded her of her mother's home-cooked meals, many of which Val tried to modify for the restaurant. They punctuated the important events of their lives. She couldn't help but wonder if Philip would enjoy those meals, too.

To do that, he'd have to stick around until at least Thanksgiving. The idea was too frightening to imagine.

The music played low and soft in the background, periodically accompanied by the sound of Nati's movements in the kitchen. She'd been good about them having dinner without interruption, and Val promised herself she'd find some way to thank her.

They ended the meal with coffee and pineapple-rum cake that Val had made earlier on a whim. Despite her excessive reaction to Philip's obvious pleasure, it had gone better than she'd thought, and she had her sister to thank for that, as well.

Val didn't want to ruin their easy time, but Philip had stopped by for a reason and it was best to just get on with it.

"I know you're not here just for the food," Val hedged.

"No, but it was certainly worth the drive."

"If you didn't drive out to our exclusive corner of the county for the rare treat of trying Puerto Rican cuisine, what *did* you come here for, sir?"

Philip wiped his lips with the napkin and set it off to the side with the other dirty dishes that Val would handle later. "I presented our proposal to my father. The good news is, he didn't reject it out of hand."

"That's a start, isn't it?" Val wanted to be optimistic. She didn't want to get into a fight with anyone over this, especially if it put her and Philip on opposite sides of the issue. They'd worked so well together, and she wanted to continue to do so.

"Yes, but he isn't entirely convinced. He's afraid we'll lose investors because none of this was in our original plan."

"And you? What do you think?"

"It's a realistic fear but I don't think people will pull out. Most projects have to consider the community's interests or they don't get approved. It's my father. He's not big on compromise."

"So it is bad news?" Val said, her stomach twisting in anxiety. "He's going to turn it down?"

"I don't believe so. I'm almost certain he'll agree, if for no other reason than to head off any delays."

Philip reached his hand out to take hers. She hesitated, unable to forget how his touch sent a million ripples of pleasure across her skin. The memory of it made her hunger for it, and everything that came with it. Everything she shouldn't want right now.

But he was a self-destruct button she couldn't help but press.

She turned her hand so that his palm settled into the cradle of hers. Her eyes flicked up to meet his gaze.

"So?" she whispered.

He blinked rapidly, as if waking from a trance. "I have an idea that might help him cross over to our side."

"And here I thought you were both on the Dark Side."

His laughter destroyed the tension but he didn't let her hand go. He leaned forward, giving her what he probably thought was his best evil glare, but instead he came off looking like he was a bit gassy. "You won't know until you cross over, will you?"

He was too cute to look fierce. "Ha, ha. Okay, Darth Meanie. You're avoiding the subject. What's your idea?"

"Darth Meanie. Hmm, not the fiercest Sith name ever." Philip straightened. Val took the opportunity to let her hand slide out of his before she got used to it, because she liked holding his hand way too much.

"My mother is holding a fundraiser. I think it would be a good idea if you came."

Maybe she hadn't heard him right. "Why would my going to a fundraiser I probably can't afford to participate in be a good idea?"

"Because, it'll be a chance to meet my father and talk to him about the proposal. Plus, the food is usually excellent and there are always some interesting personalities. Speaking of which, Étienne and Malena will be there, as well."

"You had me at the food," she quipped before growing serious. "I guess it also means your dad will be mellow. More inclined to listen to someone like me."

Philip frowned, studying her as if trying to understand something. "Not someone *like* you. Just you.

He'll listen because you're not a person that anyone can ignore."

"You think I can be persuasive based on the sheer force of my personality?" Val scoffed, and crossed her arms, hugging herself.

Philip shook his head, his frown deepening. He might not be able to pull off mean, but he could do displeasure just fine. "How can you have any doubts about yourself? Granted, I don't know you as much as I'd like, but we've been working together lately and I think I know you well enough." He paused, still leaning forward on the table, his gaze intense.

"You're honest, almost to a fault," he continued. "You're not afraid of hard work. You're intelligent to the point of being intimidating. You're funny, but also serious when you need to be." Val snorted softly at that, but he had ensnared her with his words and she was utterly under his spell. "You never make a decision without thinking about everyone it could affect, and never expect anything in return." He paused, hesitating on his own words before plunging ahead. "And you are so beautiful, sometimes it's like a punch in the gut to look at you."

Everything fell silent. The music receded. Even the bustling in the kitchen that had served as the soundtrack to their dinner disappeared until only his words hung in the air. Val stared and stared because she didn't know what else to do.

"You think those things? About me?"

Philip nodded. "I do."

There had always been an attraction between them. A spark that, left to itself, threatened to flare up into something that could burn for a long time. But this was more; it was intense and unexpected and terrifyingly *more*.

When Val didn't answer right away, Philip cleared his throat and added, "My father is no idiot. He won't help but be taken by you."

She wanted to say something. Anything. It was a lot, and her nonreaction clearly had an effect on him, if the way his eyes shifted away from hers was any indication. "Philip, I—"

"Hey, I'm done back here." Nati's voice was an explosion of sound as she crossed the restaurant area. "You need anything else before I get out of here?"

"Oh, uh, no," Val said, shaking herself out of the stupor Philip's words had created. "We're fine."

Philip snapped out of his daze, as well. "It was nice to meet you."

"Me, too." Nati paused, glancing at both of them before she spoke up again. "And I appreciate your help with this stuff happening in the neighborhood. It means a lot to us. We were a little hopeless a few months ago, but Val's been so optimistic lately about the work you're doing together."

"I'd love to take credit, but Val, uh, the advocacy group has been instrumental, as well."

"And yet it'd be meaningless if no one was listening. So thanks for listening." Nati turned her gaze on Val. "See you upstairs." She winked, a promise that she would have a lot more to say as soon as she got Val alone.

When Nati left, the silence returned. Val worried her fingers on her lap, and, to Philip's credit, he left her to her thoughts, watching her as he sipped his water. He'd said so much, she hadn't processed it all, so her mind hinged on the one thing it could handle. The situation in East Ward was a much easier problem for her to solve than that of her feelings and how they'd smashed together without any hope of disentangling them. Philip had offered her an opportunity she would be foolish to turn down.

"Okay. I'll go."

A smile split his face, the kind that had made Nati's brain crash and burn earlier. "*We'll* go. And we'll talk to him together. I'll be with you the whole time."

She didn't bother to point out that they'd gone from zero to social in less than sixty seconds, and to meeting his parents, no less. The meeting-the-parents part alone would strike fear in anyone's heart. This fact, as well as her feelings, would have to be dealt with later.

"I guess Cinderella has a ball to get ready for."

Chapter Eighteen

There was nothing more stress inducing than inadvertently confessing your feelings for someone and having that person say exactly nothing in return.

Nevertheless, Philip was happy Val had accepted his invitation to come to the fundraiser. Meeting her might help win his father over, if only because he couldn't continue to be indifferent to the people in the community if he actually got to know them. At least, that was the excuse Philip gave himself when he'd latched onto his mother's suggestion. Persuade his father to cooperate. Right, got it.

Because his father had never, in all the years he'd been doing this work, conceded to a community's wishes for adjustments in design or housing accessibility? He'd never had to negotiate about the infinite number of details in a development project? Of course, he had. This was not his father's first or even fiftieth rodeo.

Philip had to acknowledge that his father was already inclined to cooperate, if only because the proposed changes were so common sense, it would be bad business not to agree to them and risk having the city block the project just as they were so close to starting. And it was the right thing to do. You'd have to be a doorknob not to see that.

So the truth was, he invited Val to the fundraiser because he wanted to spend time with her. Take her on another quasi date. Watch her glee as she tasted all the delightful things his mother had likely planned for the dinner. Have an excuse to dress up and dance badly with her and hear her make a joke or observation about something he wouldn't have dreamed of seeing the way she did. No wonder he'd vomited his feelings all over her.

She'd been so stunned, she'd had nothing to say in return.

She'd accepted the invitation anyway, because it would serve her purpose. She had always been clear about what her motivation was for engaging with him ever since she'd found out who he was. Unlike him, she'd never lied.

So when he drove up to her building and stepped out to ring her doorbell the night of the fundraiser, there was no reason for his stomach to be twisted in knots. He had no reason to worry about his appearance, which even he had to admit was pretty damned impeccable. And there was absolutely no reason for his heart to be pounding as if it were going to leap out of his chest and run off into the night. That was not what he was here for.

Except that when the metallic buzz of Val's doorbell reverberated within, and the fluorescent bulb in the corridor flared to life like a clutch of fireflies, he felt like it was prom night all over again. He stepped back when the door opened, the light illuminating her from behind, and his capacity for flimsy rationalizations disappeared. Words gnarled in his throat and all that came out was, "Wow."

Val turned away, hiding a small smile. The green fabric drew light from the earthy undertones of her skin, making her appear illuminated from within. Her curls, the ones he wished he could bury his fingers in, were neatly tucked up, two perfect ones dangling like strings of dark pearls around her face, exposing a long neck bedecked by her ever-present rosary. His eyes raked over her, unable to find a place to rest because every single part of her demanded his attention.

"Val," he said, her name an ache in the middle of his chest. He lost all track of his heart—maybe it had already left his body.

She took a step toward him, stumbling on her golden heels, and was suddenly in his arms.

"I got you." He hadn't held her since they'd last danced together, and in his opinion, in his arms was right where she needed to be. Nothing had changed since that first time except how much he wanted her, a need that was growing to unbearable proportions.

"It's like a movie," she said, her words suffused with that hint of humor she wasn't afraid to turn on herself. "Girl undergoes transformation, girl almost falls on her face. Boy catches her."

"What happens afterward?"

She straightened, smoothing out the nonexistent wrinkles of her dress. "If the writers are fair, the boy would fall, as well."

No problem there. This boy had already fallen. "I'll try not to fall on you."

Val smirked, her eyes glittering with her wicked humor, and he prepared himself for it. "In that tuxedo, you could stumble any way you want, and you'd still look good."

He opened the passenger door with a shaky hand, easing her into his inconveniently low car. "You're getting soft. I wasn't prepared for a compliment."

"Oh, don't worry. The burn will come. Now get in and distract me before my anxiety takes over."

Philip slid into the driver's seat and turned to face her before starting the car. "Look, I know I invited you with the intention of meeting my father. But I don't want you to feel so much pressure that it ruins your night. We can just forgo that part and enjoy ourselves. These things can be a lot of fun if you're with the right company." He turned on the engine, and the car hummed to life. "And you, Ms. Navarro, are in the best company."

"Wow, put a man in black and he thinks he can take over the galaxy."

"That's right. Don't you forget it."

Val laughed, easy and relaxed. Settling in for the unpredictable drive that could take them ten minutes or forty-five, depending on the traffic over the bridge, she asked, "So, what can I expect at one of these events?"

"There are usually speeches to thank donors, a silent auction, that sort of thing, but at its core, it's a party. Half the fun is seeing which celebrities show up. I think you'll enjoy it."

"I'm sure I will," she sighed, betraying a hint of unease. "Once I meet your father, I'll be able to relax and enjoy myself."

"Then we'll make sure to get that out of the way as soon as possible."

"You'd better." Val smiled as she reached for the satellite radio buttons but stopped just short. He realized she was waiting for his permission.

"Of course you can turn it on," he said. "You probably have better taste in music than I do."

"Some people are weird about that."

"I'm weird, but not about that."

The sound of her laughter was drowned out by a classic rock ballad streaming through the car speakers. Val listened for a moment, then shook her head.

"Nice, but not quite the mood I'm looking for." She fiddled with the buttons until the nearly operatic opening of "If I Can't Have You" filled the interior.

"Wait a minute. I love this song!" To his surprise, Val let out a whoop of laughter before rolling down their windows and launching into a more-than-respectable sing-along. The wind as they crossed the bridge whipped inside the car, endangering their carefully styled hair, but Val could care less, so Philip decided not to care, either.

He didn't know all the lyrics, but out of a vague memory of having heard it on repeat somewhere, he recognized the refrain and joined in.

Flying across the Verrazano Bridge, with New York City sparkling like a constellation in front of them, he brought up the backup each time the song launched into the refrain, but then lapsed into a garbled hum-along to allow Val to take the solo.

He'd once told Val he preferred to have company on pleasure drives and this ride was exactly what he'd always envisioned. Someone like her, alive with her own fears and anxieties, but willing to take them on in the face of things she didn't know. To get dressed up on the flimsiest of excuses and go to a party where she knew all of four people and still have the energy and joy to raise her voice and sing as loud as the wind permitted. A person who, if she felt half of what he felt when he was with her, was willing to deny herself in the service of what she believed to be right, even if it meant holding back and saying no to something that could bring her happiness.

When confronted with someone like that, no one could fault him for falling in love with her.

The question was, could she ever feel the same way about him, given the circumstances?

Chapter Nineteen

The prospect of meeting Philip's father had Val's insides mushed up like a plate of mofongo, though their wild sing-along had gone a long way toward calming her down. These were very rich people, used to socializing with other very rich people. She'd never been to an event like this and had no idea what to do or how to act. Val was more than just a fish out of water—she was an entirely different species altogether.

She wasn't completely adrift. She had Philip and he'd promised not to abandon her. This might be his crowd and he might have grown up in a different environment, but Val usually forgot that he was wealthy. Except for dinner at Coq au Vin, or whenever she paid extra attention to his perfectly tailored suits. But he never acted like he was anything other than himself. A super geek wrapped up in a super-hot package.

They arrived at a cordoned off section of the street, where a dapper valet dressed in a short red coat and black pants took Philip's keys. Val eased herself very carefully out of his car—knowing her, she'd tear her dress right up to her waist and give up the game before it had even started.

Philip placed a hand on her elbow and glanced up at the building. Val followed his gaze to the roof, where spotlights lunged up into the sky and people circulated to the distant sound of music. "The fund-raiser is being held up there," he explained.

She whistled at the sight. "That looks like one serious party."

"My mother's fundraisers tend to be popular, especially when they involve an auction."

"What's being auctioned?"

"The usual—a hotel stay, art, an exclusive vacation—whatever the donors decide to contribute."

Val nodded, imagining the kind of money that was being thrown around at an event like this. "It sounds like your mom makes a killing."

Philip smiled. "She's good at what she does."

He led her inside the building and Val had to scoop her jaw off the floor. She'd only seen hotels like this on television—fabulously dressed people in vast rooms that were so polished, the glare was blinding. She took in the sleek marble floors, soaring stone columns and even a winding staircase, which they passed on their way to elevators that slid up to the top of the building inside glass tubes that coruscated light.

The elevator doors opened onto a fairy tableau. Strings of light formed a latticework over a massive outdoor banquet arrangement. Fine linen tablecloths, silverware and crystal adorned the tables. Giant screens peppered the enclosed auction area, where people milled around descriptions of the auction items.

But dinner would be served outdoors, under the moon and the lanterns on this clear, cloudless night. It was like nothing she'd ever seen before.

She clutched Philip's arm. "I can't do this."

Philip swept the perfectly coiled hair away from her face and gently lifted her chin. "Yes you can."

"These are your people. You know how to act around them."

"So do you, Val. They aren't extraterrestrials."

Panic crawled up her throat, threatening to choke her. "They're going to catch the stench of my middle class and toss me off the roof."

"Val!" Philip blurted out before laughing so hard, tears squeezed out of the corners of his eyes. Her panic turned to laughter as well until she was nearly doubled over with it.

"Fine, okay. Don't laugh at me. I was just spiraling for a minute. I'm good." She took a deep breath before repeating, "I'm good."

Philip pulled her gently against him. "You're more than good. You look delectable, the type of woman a man would dream of having on his arm."

Delectable. That word sent a discharge of heat somewhere south of her belly button. The *bruja* seated in the impulse control center of her brain shouted something at her, trying to remind her of the dangers around her, but she ignored her.

She was tired of being afraid.

"Philip, you made it!"

Val turned to see an elegant, older woman approaching. She seemed to blaze with the radiance of the lanterns surrounding them. Her golden hair was swept soft and loose over the midnight blue sleeves of an elegant evening gown. Layers of delicate tulle and satin flowed from a fitted waist, while the bodice was embroidered with finely stitched, whorled designs. Val didn't have to wonder who she was. Philip's face was an echo of this woman's, and they had the same eyes the color of lapis lazuli.

Under normal circumstances, meeting Philip's parents would be monumental. People planned for these things. Val so wanted to get this right.

"Ma, this is Val. Val, my mother, Grace Wagner."

"I guessed as much by the resemblance," Val said, offering her warmest smile, chasing away the urge to collapse in on herself. This was not the time to be shy. "It's such a pleasure to meet you, Mrs. Wagner."

Grace's eyes crinkled at the edges, much like Philip's did when he smiled, and Val found comfort in the resemblance. "You may call me Grace, darling. My, my, that dress color is absolutely stunning on you," she purred with a slow, Southern drawl.

"Let's make introductions and get you both seated." Grace tucked her hand in the crook of Val's arm, leading her into the dining area. Philip paused every now and again to greet people they knew and introduce them to Val, while Grace charmed them with a combination of quick wit and familiarity. Val had been so terrified that she'd have to generate conversation points to speak to people, but Grace lived up to her name, handling everything with the ease of long practice.

"You'll be seated near me and my husband. You can speak to him whenever the opportunity presents itself."

Val stiffened in surprise. "I guess Philip told you about our work."

Grace squeezed Val's hand. "He shares a lot with me, and from what he's told me, he's very proud of what you've both accomplished." She glanced at Philip, who flanked Val on her opposite side. "Did you warn her about the speeches?" Grace asked.

"Yes, including the one you're giving," he retorted.

"And to think I was just now talking you up. Pest," she scolded without bite. To Val, she said, "I find that copious amounts of champagne help ease the agony." She plucked two fluted glasses from a passing server and handed one each to Val and Philip. "There will be live music after and—oh, dear—is that Mavis Richards?" Her gaze flicked beyond Val and Philip to someone in the distance. "I didn't invite her. She must be someone's plus one. I have to find out who. If you'll excuse me."

"And there she goes," Philip said as she floated away.

"Your mom seems like a lot of fun," Val said before a familiar voice greeted her from the other side of their table. Étienne was already on his feet and making his way to greet them.

"Val! You are even more of a vision than usual. How did you get tied up with this frog?"

"You're supposed to be on my side," Philip protested.

Étienne took Val's hand, the gesture eliciting a giggle that she couldn't hold back. "I am always on the side of beauty." He brushed his lips ever so lightly across her knuckles. "It is a pleasure to see you again."

Philip looked past him at their table. "Where's Malena?"

Étienne's exuberant demeanor faltered, and Val had to repress the urge to ask him if he was okay. "She had other plans this evening."

The shift in Étienne's mood was hard to miss. But the out-in-the-open venue made heartfelt exchanges difficult, and Étienne recovered his good humor quickly enough. "That means Val will have two admirers at her feet."

Val played along, batting her lashes. "It's what every woman dreams of."

"Okay, enough of that," Philip said over their shared laughter.

They settled in, drinks and cocktails appearing before them. The seat next to Val remained empty, taunting her, but she wasn't going to let it ruin her night.

By her second glass of champagne, Val was so relaxed, she barely noticed the comings and goings of the table until Philip stood to shake someone's hand. She looked up, up, up at a man who was at least as tall as Philip. Philip introduced his father.

"A pleasure, Mr. Wagner," Val said, hoping she came across as charming. Philip was, in fact, the spitting image of his mother, but there something in the older Wagner's height and the severity of his features that she recognized in Philip.

Étienne led the banter at their table, to Val's relief. Philip's mother was right—the speeches were a snooze-fest only mitigated by the champagne, Étienne's wicked expressions and Philip's warm arm around her shoulder. They lasted forever, but Val found herself shifting ever so slowly into the heat of Philip's body and pulled away, reminding herself of what she was supposed to be doing here.

Her gaze shifted to Philip's father, but he was politely absorbed in pretending to care about what was being said. She hadn't exactly been presented with the opportunity to speak to him so she put that out of her head for the moment, relieved when the speeches finally ended and the appetizers appeared.

Now food was something she could get into.

Val scanned the offerings, finally settling on the fig and goat cheese phyllo pocket. She moaned at the delicate interplay of sweet and salty flavors.

Philip placed another pocket on her plate. "Let me guess. Cheese?"

Val moaned again around her mouthful. "Always the cheese."

"You seem to be enjoying your appetizer," Andreas observed.

Val swallowed. She knew this was her chance, but she was sorry to break the intimate moment she was having with her meal.

"Food is central to my life." Val said, taking a sip of water. "I own a restaurant in East Ward. You might be familiar with the area."

Andreas's ice-blue eyes flickered toward Philip. "Is that where Philip met you?"

Philip answered, "She's actually a committee chair for the East Ward Fair Housing Coalition."

Andreas's expression shuttered, his face growing impassive. "I see. So I can partly thank you for the proposal Philip presented to me."

Val smiled. "I'd like to think it was a group effort. We all worked very hard on it and tried to take everyone's interests into account." Val thought of the anger she once felt toward Wagner Developments, how she wanted to set it all on fire. But after Philip and the work they'd done together, she didn't feel nearly as peeved. "Especially your team."

Andreas raised his eyebrows in surprise. "How so?"

Val set her fork down and shifted in her chair. "I have to confess. I was angry when your company bought the Victoria and was afraid of the changes your company might bring to our community. Especially when the evictions started."

She perceived the tension coming from the older man, who possibly expected an attack and was preparing for a counteroffensive. He reminded her so much of Olivia in that moment, so quick to come out swinging. She had to head that off.

"But when Philip demonstrated how willing he was to communicate with us, I realized it was key to making sure everyone's needs were met. The Victoria was a fluke in Wagner's business practices, a question of having an objective without really taking into account all the stakeholders. I mean, you didn't even have a liaison to the community when that project was taken on."

"You're right. There didn't seem to be a need on such a small project," he said, his hackles visibly lowering.

"But we applied those lessons to the more ambitious waterfront project. I think with the new plan in place, things will go much more smoothly and without the delays that have plagued the Victoria.

And that's a win for everyone, don't you think, Mr. Wagner?"

Andreas watched her, which made Val feel like a pinned butterfly about to be poked by a scientist. Out of the corner of her eyes, she observed Étienne, who seemed to be absorbed in their every word, and Philip, who wore a look of pride. He placed a hand on her thigh and gave it a squeeze.

"Please call me Andreas. I have a few questions for clarification, if both of you don't mind." He glanced past Val to include Philip.

Val wanted to fist-bump the air but folded her hands in her lap instead as Philip answered, "Ask away."

Val spent a good part of dinner engaged in pleasant conversation with Philip's father, answering his questions about the proposal. Whenever she wasn't able to clarify a point outside of her area of expertise, Philip stepped in to help her out.

When dinner was over, there was dancing, which Val got her fill of by partnering with Étienne or Philip, and sometimes with both at the same time. They experienced three celebrity sightings, which Val couldn't wait to tell Nati about when she got home.

As Philip had promised, it really was just a grand party in the end. Val couldn't remember when she'd had so much fun and it was only due to sheer exhaustion that the three of them parted ways to go home for the night.

"You know what I realized?" Philip asked after they'd driven back to her place and he parked, this time on the cross street at the curb, just under her apartment.

"What did you realize?" she answered.

"Every time we go out, our dates revolve around food."

Val smiled, shaking her head. "You didn't tell me this was a date."

Even in the car's dim interior, Val caught the hint of Philip's blush. His mouth opened and closed a few times before he said, "You know what I mean."

She'd been keeping him at bay since he told her who he was, certain that if she gave him half a chance, he'd hurt her, prove to her that her trust was misplaced. But it felt like an old refrain from a song that she'd been listening to on repeat for too long.

Maybe this time, it would be different.

"I'm okay with calling tonight a date."

Philip turned slightly to face her, and he'd never seemed so vulnerable. "You are?"

Val reached over the black leather armrest and took his hand. His shock was evident in the way his eyebrow quirked upward. But he didn't resist, watching her with quiet intensity as she turned his hand palm up and slowly, without breaking eye contact, pressed a kiss to it. She lingered there, tasting the sharp flavor of salt and hand soap, while the crease of his palm against her lips was like a return kiss. She pulled back slowly, folding his fingers closed over her phantom gift.

His shocked expression morphed into something dark, like agony. He held himself still, watching and waiting, the only hint of movement a quickening of his breathing. Of course, he would wait for her. It seemed he'd been waiting for her since the very beginning. Waiting for her to be ready, to feel safe, to finally catch up to him.

She tilted her head up, her skin tingling with the sharp edge of expectation. Caution called out from somewhere far away, urging her to slow down. But it was nothing more than a faint echo coming to her from a distance before dissipating into silence. She leaned into him and he met her halfway, their lips a whisper against each other. He kissed her gently, even when her lips fell open in invitation. He broke away before something more incendiary could take over.

"Val?" he asked, his voice husky with the kind of longing she recognized in herself.

She ran her hand over the smooth material of his dress shirt, his muscles twitching beneath the fabric. Warm and tense, he leaned into her exploratory touch. She brushed the skin at the nape of his neck, his soft, dark gold hair tickling her fingers. She had anticipated that her touch-starved body would react instantaneously to Philip. But the expectation was nothing compared to the hunger that gnawed at her, the need to experience the glide of sweat-slicked heat against heat making her weak and achy all over.

Burying her fingers in his dark blond curls, she tugged his head toward her, but his hand had made its way behind her head and before she could take the lead, he pulled her to him and answered her kiss, turning her blood to churning magma beneath her skin. He wasn't polite or restrained in any way. He was made of fire, too.

By the time they came up for air, she was halfway across the armrest, the gearshift a pressure on her hip that she'd been too caught up to pay attention to.

He rested his hands on her shoulders, forehead to forehead, chasing his breath with each exhale.

"Come upstairs with me," she whispered.

His face was painted with the kind of agony she wanted to prolong until they broke night again. "Val," he breathed. "Is this what you want?"

Wanting had never been her problem. "Yes."

Chapter Twenty

Val paused at the entrance of her bedroom, the immaculate space appearing small and plain after the opulence of the party they'd just left. She thought about playing it off, but her mouth was way ahead of her brain.

"I know it's not what you're used to," she said, sweeping her hand to indicate her room.

Philip's eyes, which had been alive with their shared excitement only a moment earlier, grew soft. He held her hand in his large one and squeezed it.

"This is better because it's yours." When Val didn't answer, he tugged her close to him. "If you've changed your mind and want to wait, I understand. You don't have to do anything you don't want to do."

"No!" she said, so quickly it brought a smile to his face. "I was just… Whatever, it's gone. All good."

She pulled him inside and shut the door, making sure to lock it before crossing to the opposite side of her bed and switching on a lamp, suffusing the room in its fairy-gold glow. He seemed to take up all the available space, especially in his ultra formal tuxedo, which made everything look dull in comparison.

Philip ran a forefinger over the column of her neck before capturing a lose curl. "May I undo your hair?"

Val nodded, and he made quick work of the bobby pins and nearly invisible clips, her hair tumbling like rain around her shoulders. He used both hands to run his fingers through her hair, teasing the curls into shape.

"I've always wanted to touch your hair, since the first time I met you."

"I would have never guessed. Some people have no self-restraint and just touch it without permission."

He frowned at this. "I'd never touch you without asking first."

Val wrapped her arms around his shoulders, stretching her body so she could feel every one of his hard angles and soft places. "Tonight, you have permission to touch me anywhere you want. Got it?"

"Dammit, Val," he said before pulling her flush against him and kissing her with a heat that took her by surprise. They were no longer teasing each other as each layer of clothing gave way to their roaming hands and mouths until they were down to their underwear.

"You're beautiful," he whispered. Val swallowed at the sight of the thick cluster of blond curls over his well-defined chest, turning caramel-colored in the golden light. They trailed down over his belly, disappearing beneath the elastic of his boxers, which hinted at the tantalizing swell of his erection.

"You're not too bad yourself," she answered. His face brightened momentarily before all levity disappeared again. He captured her bottom lip in his and worried it before kissing her in earnest. He wasted no time in pulling her against him, his usually measured movements blazing into a frenzy of hands stroking her skin, fingers coaxing spirals of response everywhere they roamed. Soon they were both in bed, his weight pressing her with delicious heft into the mattress.

She'd been afraid. Even now that she was prepared to do wonderful, terrible things to his body, she balked at the power he had over her.

More importantly, she feared most for her heart. A cut from him and she would not soon recover.

She quieted those thoughts, wound her legs around his waist and pulled him close. The weight of his erection pressed against her, forcing what little good sense she possessed to leave the building, with no intentions of returning.

Philip nestled into her thighs, still unable to believe that he was actually here with her in this way. He held her gaze as he ground against her, his hardness sliding against the slick heat that soaked through her underwear.

"Philip, please...please keep doing that..." Her breath hitched on each word. The intensity of her kisses, the gyration of her hips under his, sent bolts of electricity exploding along his back and legs. Each time she moved, she wound him up like a fairground doll. He'd wanted her for so long that he had to bite down hard on his lip to keep himself from coming apart before she did.

When she did come undone, he was barely holding himself together.

"What the hell just happened?" she gasped, shaking in his arms.

"I think dry-humping is seriously underrated."

"Baby...you made me...and we haven't even..." She writhed beneath him, her nails digging into his skin. It really had been that long. "Come back and kiss me."

That, he could do. He kissed her before making his way down her neck and shoulders, his tongue drawing designs on her breasts and the taut, dark nipples. She was silk wherever he touched her, stoking another kind of heat, which scalded him from inside and out.

Every time she touched him, she sent him closer to the edge until he couldn't take it anymore. He grabbed her hands and pinned them over her head.

"Keep still," he rasped.

"Or else?" she breathed, and it made her ten times sexier when she sassed him this way.

"Or else I'll tie you down."

"That's really not the threat you think it is."

He laughed, and kissed her, releasing her to blaze a downward path until he reached the border of her underwear. He caught her gaze, the half smile she gave him sending another volley of electricity through him before he nudged the elastic aside. Latching onto a spot on her hip bone, he sucked on it, while his fingernails scraped the skin of her thigh. He would leave a mark, and his body answered with a powerful rush of need.

"Here, I thought you were a nice young man." She grasped fistfuls of his hair as he tugged her underwear down with deliberate slowness. Once free, she opened her knees in invitation.

"Please, Philip," she begged, and he was completely under her command. He dipped his head and savored her, her body trembling in answer. She was so responsive, so easy with giving and receiving pleasure. And when she came apart again, he knew he could become addicted to the way she loved and the knowledge that he could please her.

"My turn," she whispered when she'd come down from her high. She pushed him back on the bed and reached over, rummaging in the drawer of her end table.

"What do you have in there?" he asked.

She held the condom packet up, the silver wrapper winking in the lamplight.

"That's my secret," she teased as she tore it open and rolled it over him with exaggerated slowness, eliciting a long hiss from him. "I'm going for a little ride."

He exhaled sharply, reduced to monosyllables when she lifted herself over him and sank down on his erection. Whatever control he had left, he surrendered it to her.

She brought his hands up to cup her breasts, teaching him how she liked to be touched. He held her tight as he rammed upward, until without warning, he flipped them over and rode her in earnest.

"You are… I can't…" He dropped his head, trembling as he tried to keep himself back.

"Let go, and I'll follow."

Her words were enough to send him over the edge into free fall, her own release washing over him in waves until they subsided.

He slipped out of her and removed the condom, searching for somewhere to discard it.

"Wastebasket. Other side of the end table. Tissues on the bureau," she mumbled.

He made quick work of cleaning up before pulling the duvet over them. He tucked her in a natural spot in the crook of his arm and wrapped her in his heat. He marveled that someone as tough as she was could also be so pliant.

"That was…surprising," she said, snaking her arm over his chest, squeezing him.

"How?" he asked, muffling a yawn against his hand.

"You're so, I don't know, proper and everything and then, you're still polite but like…a little freaky, too."

He laughed. "Maybe I don't want to scare you." He rolled over onto her. "Maybe I like to take it slow before I pull out the key to my playroom."

"Damn," she purred. "That turned me on way more than it should have."

He nuzzled her neck, dragging his nose across her shoulder and kissing the tender skin of her biceps. The crease of her elbow. The muscles of her forearm before he stopped to stare down at her, his face suddenly serious.

"You're going to have to stick around if you want any part of that freakery," he said, injecting humor into his words, though what he hoped for, what he wanted, was anything but light.

"You mean, we'd get to do this again?" Val bucked her hips upward.

Philip rubbed his chin, pretending to think. "Yes. But I hope there's more than just this."

She tangled her fingers in the thick curls of his chest. "I can stick around."

"In that case," he said, dragging his nose back up to her ear. "I might even talk dirty to you."

"Dios mío."

* * *

Val blinked the sunlight away, and the night before came rushing back in all its intimate and scorching detail. The combined aroma of perfume, cologne and sex hung in air. A weight rested over her waist and something pinned her leg down. It was hot— hotter than she was used to. She shifted her leg, freeing it, and slid it out from under the bedsheets. But the weight around her waist tightened, pinning her against a chest and other hard parts.

This waking up next to Philip was something she needed to do regularly.

They were nothing more than worn flesh and strained muscles but he clearly wanted her again. He stroked her hips and sides, coaxing her body to life when, without warning, her stomach released a long rumble.

Philip pulled back, smiling down at her. "Are you hungry?"

She shrugged. "Maybe a little." Her stomach rumbled loudly again.

"Maybe a lot," he answered.

The slam of a door reverberated through the apartment, and Val shot up into a sitting position. It finally registered that it was light outside, and not particularly early in the morning, either. She grabbed her phone, which only confirmed her suspicions.

"Dammit, we overslept," she whispered. "Nati's home."

She slipped out of bed, though to do what, she

couldn't be sure. Hide out until her sister went to bed? Face her like a champ and give her something to gossip about until they entered another Ice Age? She looked to Philip, hoping for an idea, but he merely lifted himself onto his elbow, his gaze raking over her naked body as she stood. A glance at the tented sheet revealed where his thoughts stood, as it were.

"Will Nati be upset that I'm here?"

"Upset? Are you kidding me? She lives for this kind of stuff. I'll never hear the end of it." She rummaged around the room. "I need my robe."

She bent to rummage through the closet, annoyed that her robe had decided to take a walk.

"Haven't you ever had a guy over before?"

She shut the door, throwing her hands up in clear frustration. "Yes, but I'm always very careful. She's my little sister, you know? And to be honest, you staying last night was not exactly preplanned."

"Take it from someone who makes plans for a living, they are completely overrated." He stood, the blanket sliding off his naked boy. She swallowed hard as he approached and tapped her nose. "I'll hide if that's what you want. But you're hungry and you gave me quite an appetite, so we're going to have to leave your room at some point."

"I could have breakfast delivered to our room."

Philip laughed. "Why don't we start with getting dressed?"

Right. Val pulled on the first pajama set she

found—green pants and tank top covered in Baby Yodas.

Philip admired her outfit. "That's the best thing I've ever seen. Now I want to kiss you."

"First, there's a brand-new toothbrush in the bathroom drawer. Go!" she ordered. "Then we'll see."

"Of course," he said, barely repressing his laughter.

When he was done brushing his teeth, he came back out, pulled her to him and gave her the kiss he promised until they gasped for breath. He then dragged his lips along her chin and up to her ear. His fingers played a fugue along the bumps of her spine as he whispered, "Let's go face the firing squad. Ready?"

Val glared at the door. "There's no way to get ready for my sister." Short of forcing Philip to leave through the fire escape like a horny teenager, Val was going to have to woman-up and face Nati, knowing full well that everything would get back to Olivia. Yet again, she was giving them something to talk about.

At least this time, it involved Val getting laid, instead of getting dumped, so that was a qualitative improvement.

And anyway, Val was hungry. Nothing, not even facing her sister with Philip in tow, was going to get between her and breakfast.

"I'll field my sister," she said. "Will you give me a few minutes?"

"At your service."

She considered him through narrowed eyes. He was taking this all too lightly, but she found it difficult to be angry when he lay sprawled across her bed in his rumpled tuxedo shirt and pants, looking gorgeously disheveled.

"Five minutes." She opened the door to her bedroom before he could befuddle her thinking and stepped out into the narrow corridor that led to her kitchen. She glanced at the familiar wall, a mural of the Yunque, making her corridor look like she could take a step and plunge headlong into the forest, which she would've loved to do to escape her sister.

The aroma and telltale bubbling up of coffee from the *cafetera* enticed Val, though the source of her anxiety was puttering around the kitchen. Two coffee cups and a plate of sliced *pan dulce* sat on the counter while Nati sipped from her favorite mug.

"That coffee for me?" Val asked.

"You and your company." Nati took a sip from her mug without looking up. *"Sucia,"* she muttered into her drink, her face stern.

Val's face went numb. "Wha— Don't call me dirty!"

"Whatever. I happened to get off my shift early last night." She shut off the *cafetera*. "So I thought I'd sneak in, because God forbid, I'd wake you up when you're sleeping." Nati took the tea bag from her cup and dropped it in the compost bin. Val caught the aroma of chamomile. Her sister would be going to bed soon and wouldn't ruin her sleep with caffeine. "Anyway, I guess I was a little too quiet because, girl…" Nati shook her head, leaving the rest to be understood.

"Nati—" Val began, leaning weakly against the counter.

"After about an hour of trying to sleep through that—" she waved her hand, her face pinched in disgust "—I got up to make myself some tea. Now, I have sounds I'll never get out of my head again. I might need a therapist."

"I swear I didn't realize you were home," Val continued, mortified. "I'm so sorry."

Nati gave Val a withering look that made her die a thousand deaths inside. Without warning, Nati burst into hysterical laughter, setting her cup on the counter and doubling over until tears squeezed out the corner of her eyes.

"What are you laughing at?"

"Oh. My. God! The look on your face! Why didn't I take a picture?" Nati rummaged in her robe for her cell phone. "Do it again so I can take a picture."

"If you don't put that phone away…" Val calculated all the ways she could dispose of Nati's body without getting caught. "I can't believe you had me going."

Nati continued laughing, until she came up for air, wiping the tears from her cheeks. "You're so gullible… I would have gone on longer…but… I couldn't anymore… Your face!"

Val scowled at her sister as she howled with laughter.

"The only reason I knew you were with someone was because I remembered the Alpha Romeo from the last time my dude was here." Nati's easy smile evaporated as she leaned in close to her sister, dropping her voice to a whisper. "So, like, are you guys a thing now?"

Val whispered, as well. "It's a long story. Just… go easy on him, will you?"

Nati sighed. "Okay, but I'm going to need a full explanation because I don't get this at all. That enemies-to-lovers stuff is great in romance novels, but in real life…?" Nati's eyes shifted and her features brightened. "Hi, Philip."

Philip gave Val a sheepish smile. "Nati."

She cocked her head in the direction of the table. "Have a seat. I picked up *pan dulce* from the bakery this morning. Can I offer you some?"

"That's really nice of you. Thank you."

"I'll help." Val mouthed, "Thank you," as she passed by her sister. Val prepared the coffee mugs while Nati and Philip bantered easily. Nati was the most extroverted of the three siblings and her friendly manner put everyone else at ease.

Val watched her sister and her… Lover? Boyfriend? She wasn't sure what to call him, but she couldn't believe this man, who was now in her kitchen, laughing at her sister's ridiculous jokes, was the same man with whom she'd been with last night, the same man she couldn't stand to see just one month ago.

She took another sip of her coffee and caught Philip watching her. His expression was gentle but intense. He didn't break eye contact until she turned her head away. This was a lot, and she was simply grateful her sister was making it easier by behaving.

The front door clicked opened, jolting Val from her thoughts. Nati stepped out into the hallway, and a wicked grin broke across her face. Val realized too late what had her sister practically rubbing her hands in glee.

She could count on Nati to cooperate with her. She was a goofball, but she'd learned the art of diplomacy in med school. Rafi was more direct, a consequence of working with teenagers all day, and less inclined to filter himself.

"I smelled the coffee and knew you were still up. What's Val making?" Rafi said as he bent to give Nati a kiss on the cheek.

"Val didn't make breakfast," Nati said meaningfully, barely suppressing a giggle.

Philip stood just as Rafi noticed him. Rafi looked from him to his sister. "I'm Rafael," he said slowly. "And you're…?"

"Philip." He offered his hand. Rafi looked down at it, then back up at Philip before slowly shaking it.

"Philip? As in Philip Wagner?" he said, giving Val a smile that was so fake, it looked painted on.

Philip visibly swallowed but answered with a steady voice. "One and the same."

"Oh." Rafi crossed his arms, appraising him. "Didn't know you worked Sundays."

"Pardon me?" Philip asked.

"Rafi," Val warned.

"I'm just saying, you're out here on a Sunday morning. Are you trying to buy this building, too?"

Nati shoved a mug of coffee in Rafi's hand. "*Callate!* That's not why he's here, dummy." She gave him a pointed look. "Nothing at all to do with the building."

Rafi looked from Nati to Val, then to Philip, then back to Val again. He must have registered Val's crazy hair, the fact that she was wearing pajamas while Philip sported a crumpled shirt and tuxedo pants.

"Well, damn," Rafi whispered before recovering himself. He turned to Val. *"Bueno, hermanita, parece que ya desajunastes..."* he said in a singsong voice, taking a sip of his coffee. Val bristled at the double entendre of him telling her she'd already had breakfast.

Val opened her mouth to put him in his place, but Nati quickly intervened. "You just coming in?"

Rafi's gaze lingered on Philip over the rim of his mug. "I was only out dancing, scandalous ones. Then Roberto and I went to an after-hour."

"Roberto?" Nati asked suggestively.

Rafi looked at Nati with extra attitude. "Nothing

like that…yet. Like I said, I leave the scandalous behavior to my big sis."

"You can quit it now," Val snapped.

"Aw, come on," Rafi said, slapping Philip's back a
little harder than necessary. "If Philip wants to hang
with us, he's gonna have to get used to being teased.
Just try not to buy our building, okay?"

Philip nodded solemnly. "Promise."

"Humph." Rafi took a seat next to Nati, not quite
taking his eyes off Philip. Val took that as a quali-
fied win.

"*¡Que jodienda!*" Nati cried out, pulling everyone's attention toward her. "What a pain! Please tell
me I wasn't the only one up all night actually being
an adult."

"Papi stayed in," Val volunteered, smiling into
her cup.

"He's sixty years old!" Nati complained. "How do
I have less of a social life than a sixty-year-old man?"

"You need to do something about that," Val said,
taking her seat.

"No way. Don't let her off the hook. It's her turn to
abstain," Rafi said. "That was me while I was working on my masters. Didn't have a minute to breathe."

"She's almost done," Val said. "And we're having
a huge party to celebrate."

Nati winked, giving Val a fist bump.

"What about you?" Rafi asked Philip, saying the
words like he was throwing down a gauntlet. "Must

have been easy for you, with your dad being rich and all."

The tension in the air was sharp and thick. Val held her breath, but Philip set down his mug and grew thoughtful. "Actually, he wasn't born rich. He's the kind who believes if he had to work for it, so do I." Philip broke a corner off his bread. "He doesn't know the meaning of the phrase 'free pass.'"

Rafi hummed. He was doing a lot of that, and there was a world of meaning behind the sound. "You know, maybe that was his way of keeping you from being a spoiled brat."

"Or maybe it's because he struggles with authentic human relationships that aren't filtered through the lens of work."

Val nearly choked on her coffee. Nati and Rafi gave each other a look that spoke volumes.

"That was really...real," Rafi said, refilling Philip's mug with the last of the coffee.

Val exhaled in relief. Philip had survived a round of the Navarros. She squeezed his hand beneath the table and joined in the general banter until Nati gave a wide yawn.

"Okay, kids, I'm off to bed. Last night's shift wiped me out."

"Leave everything. I'll clean up," Val said.

"Nope," Rafi said, collecting the empty mugs in one swift motion. "I got 'em. Nati, go to sleep. You look dead on your feet." He indicated with his head toward both Val and Philip. "You two, go do something fun." He waggled his eyebrows at Val, who rolled her eyes in response. "When I'm done, I'll check on Papi and take a little nap. I got tests to grade."

"Thanks, *bonito*," Nati said, giving him a kiss on his cheek, which Val repeated on his other side. He then turned to Philip and offered him his hand, which caught Philip by surprise, but only for a moment before returning the gesture.

Chapter Twenty-One

Val retreated to her father's office to do paperwork, the sound of banging pots, running water and clinking glasses forming the familiar background noise that she'd been listening to all her life. She sorted receipts, stopping every now and again to respond to a message from Philip. It killed her productivity but it also made her happy, so the trade-off was an acceptable one. Philip's father had accepted the proposed community benefit agreement, which meant it would be finalized and ready to present at the upcoming hearing.

They'd get together again this weekend, this time at his place. Much as Val loved her family, she was not looking forward to a repeat of their walk of shame.

She smiled again when her cell phone vibrated, but it was a call from the loan officer, Mr. Graham. It had been such a long process, putting in an offer, checking certificates, permits and other endless due diligences. And that was all before the mortgage application. Val hoped for good news, so they could be done with it and call the building her own. She imagined the surprise on Philip's face when she told him she was the new owner of this building. She took the call with her fingers crossed.

"Mr. Graham. I'm glad to hear from you."

"Likewise, Ms. Navarro," he answered, always polite and competent, which was something Val could appreciate. They exchanged a few pleasantries, which she endured with patience, eager as she was to finalize the sale of the building.

"Ms. Navarro. Val." The way he way said her name put Val on edge and the euphoria she felt when she answered the call drained away. "I apologize, but I'm afraid your application has been declined."

Her field of vision contracted, fixed on the calendar with Father Pius hanging on the opposite wall next to the portrait of her mother. "Denied? Why were we denied?"

"There were some irregularities in your credit card payment history that our system flagged. I'm sorry."

"We went over everything before submitting our application," Val said, trying her best not to sound petulant. "Why is this coming up now?"

Mr. Graham was all business, while Val's world was coming apart. "Preapprovals are not a guarantee of financing."

"I know, but I had this application reviewed. There was nothing that should've resulted in a rejection."

Mr. Graham's response came in clipped tones. "I assure you, we maintain the utmost rigorous lending requirements."

"Sounds arbitrary to me," Val muttered. Something about the whole thing didn't add up.

"I understand you're upset. Your family has been our customer for thirty years and we value your patronage—"

Val snorted but he continued. "You are invited to apply again in twelve months, when the payment under question is no longer an issue."

"If I do that, the property won't be available anymore. No, I'll be taking my business elsewhere. Have a good day."

Val shut her phone off and set it down to avoid the temptation to throw it at something. Felicia had had a colleague review the assets and income and he'd given the application the highest probability for approval. That application had not been rejected on its own merits.

Val's mind spun as she thought about the larger picture. There were only three stakeholders to whom the building might matter—the Navarros, the Gutierrezes and Wagner Developments.

Val sat up straight in her chair. Had she been steamrolled? The mortgage process was supposed to be confidential. Who would want that building so badly, they'd be willing to bend rules that, when broken, could get them in a world of trouble? And who would have the money and influence to get out of those problems if they were caught? Who could afford the audacity of interfering with her application?

Gripping her mother's crucifix. Val picked up her phone again, this time dialing Philip's number.

"Val," he said after the first ring. Despite her cross-eyed anger, she would never get used to the intimate way he said her name.

"Philip, listen, I need to ask you something."

"Go ahead."

She explained everything about putting an offer on the building nearly a month ago, as well as her conversation with Mr. Graham.

Philip was quiet for several seconds. "You put a contract on the building and you didn't tell me?"

Val leaned back in her chair, the leather squeaking in protest. "No, I didn't."

"Why?"

She didn't like the turn the conversation had taken. "Isn't it obvious? Your company is dead set on buying this entire block. I didn't want to do anything that might ruin my chances of getting this building."

"Essentially, you didn't trust me not to use this to my advantage." Philip sighed and she could see him rubbing his face the way he did when he was confused or frustrated.

"It isn't you I don't trust. This is about not letting your company take advantage of the situation for its own gain, like what just happened to my application."

"You think Wagner Developments might have something to do with your mortgage denial."

"Are you saying it's impossible?"

"I wish I could say that it was, but these things aren't unheard of." She heard shuffling on the other end of the line again. Val was afraid he might rub the skin off his face. "If something happened on our side, I'll fix it. But, Val...after everything, why do you still believe you can't trust me? I could have helped you." Philip paused before adding, "I've stepped up, tried to show you that I'm not who you think I am. Gone to bat for you—"

"Because it was the right thing to do."

"Yes, but also because I care about you. I want to be with you. And all this time, you thought I was capable of taking advantage of you. I'm not Luke."

Val's temper snapped. He was not going to turn around what was practically a crime against her into a pity party about his insecurities. "There is no reason to bring up my ex."

"Then who should I blame for your inability to trust me?"

"Philip..." She could barely say his name, it was starting to hurt too much.

They were both quiet for a long while until Philip spoke again. "I lied about who I was, and that lie has poisoned everything between us."

"No. I mean, maybe?" she whispered, but it sounded like denial to her. "I'm just trying to protect my family's home and livelihood. I can't risk that just because I caught feelings for you." Val was out of her chair and pacing. "If things don't work out, I don't have a fallback. I don't have anyone who can write me a check and bail me out. I've got myself and my family and that's it."

"I know you don't believe me, but you also have me. I'm on your side. One hundred percent."

Val stopped her pacing. Her mind whirled again. She accepted his willingness to support her on an intellectual level, but her feelings were having a hard time catching up.

"I want to believe that so badly," she said finally.

Philip sighed. "I'll look into this. But, Val, we're not going anywhere if you can't trust me. I don't know how else to show you that you can."

"I will trust you as soon as Wagner Developments stops screwing around with me."

Philip's silence was so absolute, Val thought he might've hung up on her. Instead, she heard the slow intake of breath. "I am not my company."

This was exactly the kind of thing she'd been trying to avoid. She'd let her feelings cloud her purpose. Now she was too exposed, too flayed open because she'd let herself become emotionally vulnerable. And now, her family stood to lose everything.

She could never let that happen again.

"It doesn't matter if you are your company or not. Our interests aren't the same. I don't think this is going to work."

"So that's it? You're not even going to try to work things out?"

"We tried, didn't we?"

Philp didn't say anything else and Val took it as confirmation.

"Goodbye, Philip." She ended the call, shoving the phone away from her as if it would set her hand on fire.

When she sank down into the office chair, her hands were trembling while tremors spread through her body. Her chest locked up. The tension squeezed her in iron bands, forcing the air from her lungs. She broke into a sweat, then shivered when goose bumps appeared. Cold. Hot. Burning, then freezing. And all the while, shattering into a thousand pieces.

She hadn't had a panic attack since the night Luke had humiliated her in front of everyone, and before that, when her mother died. But now she sat doubled over in her chair, attempting to take long, deep breaths while forcing her heart to slow its maniacal galloping.

Disaster scenarios plagued her. Developers taking over her building. Raised rents. Evictions. The forced closure of Navarro's. Her neighborhood changed beyond recognition, as if it was disposable, as if what was already here wasn't worth nurturing. No longer having Philip in her life—

"Stop!" Val shouted, swiping at her tearstained face. "What the hell!" She bent her head between her knees and counted to ten. Breathed deeply. Tried to still her racing heart. She needed to calm down first, talk to her family and regroup. There were other banks in the world and not all of them would be in Wagner's back pocket. They could still make this purchase happen.

And as for Philip, well, she had to put her feelings about him aside and resolve the issue with this building. The consequences if she didn't were impossible to imagine.

So Val did what she always did. Put the well-being of her family ahead of everything else, whatever the cost to her personally.

Chapter Twenty-Two

Philip let himself into his parents' town house, the dread that had been weighing him down ever since his phone call with Val receding before the instinctive relief of being in his family home. He reviewed their conversation, the deep hurt he'd felt when she'd basically admitted to not trusting him when every decision he'd made since telling her his identity was designed to win her trust.

But it was hard to mount an argument in favor of trusting him if his father was going to undermine everything Philip had done.

Philip breathed in the familiar scent of fresh flowers that his mother loved so much. The immaculate mirrors and wood surfaces comforted him with their neatness. Elegance warred with intimacy, the aloof perfection of paintings existed alongside fun, candid pictures of him and his family, all arranged in precise order. This was his family, in all their hyperorganized glory, a contrast to the chaotic warmth that characterized Val's family photographs.

Grace met him in the corridor with open arms, but her smile evaporated when she caught his expression.

"Darling, what is it?"

Philip melted into her embrace. "How do you always know how I'm feeling?"

"I'm your mother. It's what I do. Are you okay?"

He gave a tight shake of his head. "Has Dad arrived from the airport yet?"

She smoothed a curl from his forehead. "He's in his office, organizing his things."

"I need to see him."

"Just go on up. You won't be disturbing him."

Philip gave her a quick squeeze of the hand before taking the stairs. His father looked up when Philip opened the door.

"Come in, son. I wasn't going to debrief you on my trip until tomorrow, but now is as good a time as any," Andreas began, but Philip put his hand up.

"I'm looking forward to hearing all about it. But first, I need to ask you about something."

Andreas stopped shuffling his papers and pointed to the chair opposite his desk. "Have a seat."

Philip sat down. He was a mess of nerves and anxiety. He hated having to ask his father if he'd essentially committed a crime. But he had to do it because he had promised Val, and no matter where they ended up after this situation, he was committed to doing the right thing.

"You know that mixed-use you were talking about a few weeks ago. The one you said went under contract?"

"Do you have an address or lot number?"

"You didn't say at the time but I'm going to venture a guess. Does the corner of Muñoz Marin Boulevard and Clemente Avenue ring any bells with you?"

Andreas leaned back in his chair, steepling his fingers. "Ah, yes. It went under contract about a month ago, pending financing. But not to worry. It's not under contract any longer."

Philip's stomach turned sour. "Why?"

"My understanding is the buyer was not approved for financing."

He took a deep breath, the bile now somewhere in his throat. Val was right. She had been steamrolled. "And how do you happen to know all of this?"

Andreas shrugged, undoing a cuff link to roll up his sleeve. "It's a small world, Philip. You know that. The bank manager and I go back many years."

"Dad," Philip groaned. "Do you realize how illegal that is?"

Andreas dropped his hand and leaned forward in his chair. "It was a weak application. Probably saved the buyer a foreclosure down the road."

"Are you even listening to yourself? Do you have

any idea who that buyer is? Or what the circumstances are behind that purchase?"

"It's not my job to know that."

"Well, I happen to know. That application you interfered with belongs to Val Navarro. Do you remember her from the fundraiser? You spent over an hour talking to her at dinner."

His father's face went impassive, but there was no mistaking the way the color drained from it. "You're joking."

"I wish with all my heart that I wasn't."

Andreas stared at him and not for the first time did Philip wish his father didn't have such a damned good poker face. "I'm surprised she'd have the means to buy the property. I can't imagine the income from a small restaurant would cover the purchase value of the building."

Philip's breath came hard and fast. "That's beside the point. Not only is what you did professionally unethical, that restaurant has been in her family since they moved to East Ward and they were all pulling together to buy the building. She was within her rights to put an offer in for it, and she was the preferred buyer. There was no reason for you to interfere."

"I don't see why she can't continue to operate her restaurant, regardless of who owns the building—"

"You're not listening to me! If you could so callously block her ability to buy that building, how is she going to feel safe having the same company who sunk her application as her landlord?"

Andreas's face hardened. He was slipping into raider mode, and Philip wasn't going to be able to reason with him if he did so.

"Dad," Philip said. "Do you remember when you told me about Grandfather, how after the uprising, he brought the entire family from Slovakia to live in the United States?" It was a legendary story in their family—his grandfather selling his farmland and equipment to pay the passage for his family to come through Ellis Island and relocate in New Jersey.

Andreas looked uncomfortable. "Yes, of course. your grandfather Filip was a giant of a man."

Philip nodded. "When he came, he had just enough money to rent a little apartment in Hibernia, and little by little, he and his brother bought and flipped the rentals along the river. You remember what people used to say about him?"

Andreas looked away, showing an intense interest in his fingernails.

"He was the best landlord his tenants ever had," Philip continued.

"He was a shrewd businessman, Philip. He wasn't a bleeding heart."

"No, he wasn't, but he believed in treating people with respect. By the time you moved Wagner Developments headquarters to Exchange Place after he passed away, there were practically monuments to Grandpa Filip in the community."

Andreas leaned on his hand and he looked more like the father Philip had grown up with, the one who, no matter how late he worked, always came to his son's bedroom to wish him goodnight, even if he thought Philip was sleeping. The one who taught him that there were no free passes just because he was his father's son, but he should strive to work hard and be the best possible professional version of himself. His dad was aloof at times and pushed the concept of work ethic to its extreme limit, but Philip had to believe that deep down, he was motivated by love and a sense of fair play.

"He would have never pulled something like this. He believed in rules and he believed in people."

Andreas crossed his arms, staring at a point on his desk as he listened. When Philip was done, he looked up, ice-blue eyes gone cloudy with something that might have been sadness—or shame. "You inherited more than your grandfather's name."

Philip shrugged. "I get it. It's fun to win. But not at all costs. We need to fix this."

Andreas sighed, defeated. "I'll call Mr. Graham."

Philip stood, and his father stood with him. "It would mean a lot to me if you do." Philip turned to leave, emotionally drained and physically as worn-out as if he'd just finished a grueling tennis match with Étienne.

"You really care about this young woman, don't you?"

Philip tasted salt, and he hoped he wouldn't start crying in front of his dad. This was about as emotional as they'd ever gotten, and he didn't think either of them could handle his waterworks. "I love her, Dad."

His father let out a deep sigh at that. "But," Philip continued, "that's not the only reason why I'm asking you to fix this. I want to do work I'm proud of and I can't if this is the kind of thing that goes on. If I'm meant to take over the company, I won't tolerate it."

Andreas nodded in understanding. He had his phone in hand and was already dialing. Philip thought it best to leave his father to deal with this himself. He'd do the right thing, of that Philip was certain.

Now came the hard part. He had to figure out how make Val understand. It was clear she struggled with trusting him, which hurt. But he couldn't ignore the fact that her fears were not only reasonable, but had also been confirmed, if his father's actions were taken into account. He needed to make this clear, that he understood, then determine if there was any hope for the two of them.

Philip pulled into a free spot close to the restaurant, next to a dumpster with Wagner Developments stamped on the side. If that wasn't a metaphor for his life, he wasn't sure what was.

He'd called Val as soon as he left his parents' townhouse but Val didn't answer, nor did she respond to his numerous text messages. But as he strode up the walk, he was surprised to see the restaurant lights on, despite the time of the evening. He'd barely made it up the steps when the door opened and Rafi stepped outside.

"You here to see Val?"

"If she's around."

"She's around," Rafi answered, but he didn't budge from in front of the door.

"I messaged her but I haven't been able to speak to her. I thought if I came in person—"

"She knows you've been messaging her. She's upset right now and needs space."

Philip took a deep breath, having anticipated this. "There are things I need to tell her."

"You mean about your father? What more does she need to know?"

"Rafi, she's right to be angry. I know that. But he regrets what he did and he's trying to fix it. Please, let me explain things. She can throw me out afterward if she wants."

Rafi crossed his arms over his chest. "You seem like a nice guy but I never was a big fan of you being with my sister. Nothing personal, just too many conflicting interests for it to work out."

"I don't care about any of those things."

"But they matter to her."

"I'd rather hear that from her."

Rafi got very close to Philip. "I'm not going to let you in just so you can hurt her again, so it's best if you leave now," Rafi said quietly.

Philip put his hands up, the universal sign of surrender. "I won't insist. But just like you have her back, so do I. I would never do anything to intentionally hurt her."

Rafi didn't budge, leaving Philip no other outlet for his frustration than to turn and stalk back to his car. It was only when he was inside that he realized his hands were shaking. He should have heeded the sign from the universe and taken a moment to calm down, but he turned on the car instead and peeled out of the space. The whine of metal grating on metal filled the car. He'd certainly scraped his car against the dumpster, but he couldn't care less. The car could catch fire for all it mattered and he'd be capable of doing nothing more than watching it burn.

Chapter Twenty-Three

Summer made its scorching appearance as if from out of nowhere, turning everything hot, sticky and uncomfortable. Val asked Felicia to arrange, through her own contacts, a personal interview with the local credit union. The mortgage officer proved brisk and competent, expediting the preapproval for the application. Because Val had done her due diligence during the first application, the mortgage documents were ready to sign within the week.

When everything was approved, Val called Olivia and the Gutierrezes and, together with Rafi, Nati and her dad, invited them to celebrate at a local Polish restaurant, which served a pink borscht that Papi loved. The food was excellent and the mood buoyant, but everything Val put in her mouth tasted like ash. She spoke very little and responded only when spoken to. Nati glanced often in her direction and even Olivia restrained her teasing.

The conversation progressed from the extraordinary events of the previous weeks to Rafi's plans for renovating the basement, and finally settled on the upcoming City Hall meeting.

"It's already here?" Val asked, the first thing to prompt her interest all night.

"Of course. Felicia sent us an email about it a couple of days ago," Nati answered.

Wagner Developments and EWFHC would present the community benefits agreement together with the project timeline to be approved by the city. There was no way Philip wouldn't be there—he'd been as instrumental in writing the agreement as she'd been.

Just the thought of anything related to Philip sank like lead in Val's stomach, curdling the soup she'd managed to force down. He hadn't stopped trying to reach out to her until she told him, in no uncertain terms, that he needed to give her space. Indefinitely.

Olivia, who sat next to her on the faux red velvet chair that comprised the decor of the restaurant, bumped her on the shoulder. "Hey, sourpuss."

Val reached for the roll she'd been shredding the entire meal. "I am not a sourpuss."

"Don't try to pull that with me," Olivia whispered. Rafi was talking to Eunice, gesturing animatedly, while Nati and Papi were deep in discussion with

Benito, leaving them with a brief moment of privacy. "Be happy. You are the proud owner of real estate." At Val's silence, Olivia softened her voice. "I hate to see you miserable, Darth Cupcake."

"I'm not miserable!" Val snapped.

All eyes turned toward Val. She refused to hold anyone's gaze, staring down into her bowl of cold borscht. She shouldn't have snapped at Olivia, but she'd had about enough of her love life being the biggest circus in town. She was about to get up from the table and walk home when something hit her on the head.

"What the—" She looked up in time to watch a rolled-up paper towel land next to her glass of water. Rafi and Nati smothered a laugh. Olivia had her hand over her mouth, and her father, Eunice and Benito all bit back a grin.

"A toast." Rafi stood before she could protest, one hand holding a beer bottle, the other sweeping out toward Val. "To my sister, for devising a plot to save 724 Clemente Avenue from the dastardly clutches of capitalist pirates, despite obstacles both institutional and personal. You are a warrior and we all admire you very much, even if you are crankier than a basketball fan with a losing team."

Val gave him a half smile, raising her own glass. This was what she'd always wanted—to keep her family and her community intact. But while she was overjoyed for her family, her heart was missing an important piece, and now she was too damned afraid to do anything about it.

The following week, Val entered City Hall flanked by Papi, Rafi and Nati. People milled in and out of meeting rooms and into the hallways, as part of the audience for the public meeting.

"This is a good turnout," Rafi said.

"Surprising, given how dry the details can be." Val took in the crowds, pretending not to be looking for anyone in particular.

"I don't think he's here yet," Nati whispered, nudging Val in the ribs.

"Who's not here, yet?" Val retorted.

Nati crossed her arms. They were dressed in business attire—Val in a blue pencil skirt with a white, button-down blouse, while Nati wore a beige shirt-dress that was miles better than her usual scrubs. "Oh, *por favor*. You haven't stopped looking around since we got here. I'm telling you, he's not here. His car wasn't in the parking lot."

"You're awfully invested in my relationship, you know that?" Val sighed, abandoning all her pretenses of being indifferent to Philip's absence. "Maybe he didn't come in his car."

Nati glanced over at her father. "Papi, Rafi, save me a seat, okay?"

Nati pulled Val into a side hallway where the bathrooms were located. "I'm thinking, after all of this, it might be a good idea if you had a little talk with him."

Val stared at her sister. "Are you out of your mind?"

"Usually, yes, but not about this," she said, glancing around to make sure no one overheard her. "I've never known you to back down from a confrontation."

"This is different."

"Because you're scared? Yeah, these things are scary, but you know what else is scary? Missing your shot. You care about him and even though his dad is a lot to deal with, Philip seems different."

Val bit back a welling of emotion. She was in this limbo of wanting and not wanting, wishing he would give her the one assurance no human being in the world could give her—the absolute certainty that she would never be hurt again.

Nati reached out to hug her, nearly knocking Val off-balance. "Don't get in the way of your own happiness." She hooked her arm through Val's, pointing at the open door of the hearing room. "Come on. This is what you've been working toward all this time. Go get this done."

The crowd shifted and surged as people found their seats. Nati pointed to their father and Rafi, who both gave her a thumbs-up. Val reached Felicia at the conference table, not surprised to see George Leighton and Wagner Developments' community liaison already there.

Next to her was Philip, as always, captivating in his impeccable business suit, making everyone else's attempt at formal dress look plebeian in comparison.

It didn't help her state of mind when he held her gaze and gave her that brain-melting smile. She waited for the lurch in her stomach, the ready protest for why she shouldn't stare at him, exchange awkward glances with him or linger before pulling her gaze from his. But nothing came. Instead, she remembered the ease of talking all night in her restaurant, the excitement of their walk along the boardwalk, the joy of their first night together. It was easy to hold on to her fears when he wasn't standing before her with every memory they'd ever shared coiled like a stream of rainbow-colored ribbons, tethering her to him.

"Philip," she whispered, instinctively moving toward him, but she was brought up short by the presence of his father, seated next to him.

"Ms. Navarro. It's good to see you again," he said perfectly polite, as if he wasn't responsible for aging her a whole decade with his shenanigans. If he thought being polite to her was going to cancel all the aggravation he'd given her, he clearly had no idea how long Val could hold a grudge.

"I wish I could say the same." She couldn't help but narrow her eyes at him before backing away and taking the seat next to Felicia.

"What is Andreas Wagner doing here?" Val hissed.

Felicia's eyes were bright with triumph. "Right?

After he agreed to the proposal, I figured that was the extent of his involvement, but then he requested to join the meeting. Who would've thought?"

"You don't think he's going to sabotage the proposal, do you?"

"Val," Felicia whispered in return. "Where do you get such ideas?"

Wouldn't she like to know?

Val leaned back. The good news was, she had very little to present and could let Felicia take the lead, leaving her to observe Philip.

The call to order drew her attention back to the front of the crescent moon–shaped desk, where the seven members of the city council's development committee, as well as the mayor, sat facing the packed room. The meeting, for all its importance, began with the procedural blandness that characterized all city business.

When their turn came, Andreas took a back seat to Philip, allowing him to fully describe the proposal details. The presentation and proposal had been sent to the council in advance so it could be reviewed and questions prepared.

"I would like to address the members of this council and the community," Philip said.

"You may, Mr. Wagner," Mayor Simone answered.

Philip turned to the crowd, the room so packed, many stood along the back wall. Val leaned forward, eager to hear how Wagner Developments would address the issues.

"Thank you, Mayor Simone. Esteemed council members. Ladies and gentlemen. We've heard your comments and explored your complaints.

"Our company's policies of the last year have not best represented our business ethic. We would like to inform the public that we have heard your concerns and we are taking steps to mitigate the damage done by the practices of the last twelve months. It's why we worked with Mrs. Morales and community leaders to come to an agreement about sustainable, profitable development that is ethical and preserves the character and well-being of the existing community, starting with the property in question. We hope the council with look favorably on the result of that work."

Someone shouted from the back, "Are you saying you're not evicting any more tenants from their homes?"

Philip nodded. "Yes. We will revoke all lease renewals of the last six months and rewrite them with the terms the community and our company have agreed upon." He turned and captured Val's gaze. "The foundation of any good relationship is trust, and Wagner Developments is willing to do whatever it takes to demonstrate its trustworthiness to the community."

Val couldn't help the smile that broke across her face. He had done everything he could to undo the damage of that first lie. The latest complication hadn't been his fault, but he'd stepped up there, as well, and somehow gotten his father to not only accept his proposal but there he was, sitting by his son's side, with the same goofy look of pride she surely had.

When the meeting adjourned, a crowd swarmed Philip. Slowly, too slowly, the meeting room emptied. Val debated whether to approach him in the middle of the melee or try to speak to him later. Nati's hand on her elbow roused her from her indecision.

"You need to stay right here."

Val opened her mouth to answer, but Philip was rounding the table in her direction.

She swallowed, her throat dry. "Hey." Her eyes flitted away from him. She couldn't trust herself to stare at him too long.

He had less self-restraint; the way his eyes raked over her made her feel like she was standing naked in front of him. She missed him—his open need, the easy way they understood each other, his husky laughter and dry humor. All the denied feelings of the past weeks crashed over her.

"How'd you get your father to come out?"

Philip gave her a smile that didn't reach his eyes. "My father had an epiphany of sorts."

Val ached to touch him. Why had she let this rift go on for so long? "You did really well. I'm proud of you."

Philip rubbed the back of his neck, disrupting the waves of blond hair that had been so meticulously styled. Val wanted to smooth each one back into place.

Before he could answer, Leighton interrupted their conversation.

"The mayor would like to introduce you to the members of the council. You are quite the darling now." He dipped his head in greeting toward Val. "I'm sorry to steal him away."

Was this it? Was this all they were going to say to each other? Val panicked and reached for him. "Philip?"

Philip's expression was apologetic as Leighton led him away. Words tangled in Val's throat and she couldn't do anything but stare at Philip's receding back as he made his way to one of the adjacent rooms.

"It's mostly a formality," a familiar voice said. Val wrestled with whether to drag Philip out of that meeting or not. "They'll accept the proposal and it will clear the way for the approval of the waterfront project."

Val blinked rapidly as she processed Andreas Wagner's words. "Why aren't you in there with him? You're the owner of the company."

Andreas nodded almost absently, as if her question was part of a bigger conversation he had been having with himself. "He's proving himself to be a better CEO than I have been. Certainly, he is the better man."

Val turned her entire focus on Andreas. Something about him had changed since they'd last spoken. He did not seem nearly as intimidating as he had been at the fundraiser. "That's an opinion we can both agree on."

Andreas nodded, taking that in, as well. "I owe you an apology, Ms. Navarro."

She was quaking inside, not in fear, but because in her fury, she had never, in a million years, expected Andreas Wagner to ever apologize to her. She waited for him to continue.

"Your property was intended to be one of our acquisitions, so your contract to buy threw those plans in disarray. But that is hardly an excuse for what I did. It was an egregious abuse of power and for that, I am sorry."

Val huffed at his words. "I really wish you hadn't done that. But it all worked out in the end."

"So you accept my apology."

She wanted to slip away, get back to her family, and analyze what just happened. "I do. Thank you."

But Andreas evidently wasn't done with her.

"Don't let what I did influence your opinion of Philip. He had nothing to do with my actions."

Val's vision blurred and she blinked the moisture away before she started bawling in front of Philip's father. "I won't."

"I mean it, not just because he's my son. He's good and deserves to be judged on his own merits."

"He does." She surprised both Andreas and herself by stepping in to give him a quick hug, which he reciprocated awkwardly. When she stepped back, she said, "I'll see you soon."

His skin flushed a light pink. "I hope so."

In a daze, Val stumbled out of the building. Nati, Rafi and her father were waiting outside for her. She blinked into the bright sun, heat burning her inside and out.

Papi studied her. *"¿Estás bien, mija?"*

"Yeah, I'm fine," she breathed. "I'm going to walk home."

Rafi fanned himself. "It's hot as hell out here."

"I know. But I need to think."

Nati sidled close to Val. "You can think on the train, too. And it's air-conditioned."

Rafi came up on her other side as if she were going to bolt into traffic. "Are you going to wait for him to come out?"

Val should have known she couldn't put anything over on them. "It's nothing I can fix here. Just get Papi home safely."

Papi chuckled. "You kids treat me like I'm a hundred years old. *Mira, mijita*, you don't have to pretend with us. We know you have Philip on your mind. Go do what you have to do. I'll keep your nosy brother and sister busy."

"We are not nosy, Papi," Rafi said in exasperation. "We are concerned."

Nati scoffed. "No, Rafi, you're concerned. I really am just nosy."

Val pulled Nati and Rafi in for a hug. "I love you guys. Now please, get out of my face so I can think, okay?"

Nati and Rafi each left a kiss on her cheek before they crossed with Papi to the subway entrance. Val had a terrible time leaving the steps of City Hall in the hopes she might meet Philip on the way out. She had no idea how long his meeting would last, and anyway, her feelings were a changing kaleidoscope of color and intensity and she needed to get them in order before she spoke to him again.

As Val covered the blocks between City Hall and her restaurant, the fog in her brain began to clear. She had doubted Philip's intentions ever since he'd told her he was a Wagner. And she had never relented in her mistrust, even after they'd been intimate. It was true that his family's company had been an endless thorn in her side, but it was also true that he was not his company.

He'd done so much to prove his trustworthiness to her, but she'd been too blind to see that, holding on to her fear of betrayal. She had to fix that as soon as she could get him alone.

Rafi was right. It was hot as hell and the humidity was quickly turning to gathering clouds, which opened up and spilled the moment she stepped inside the empty restaurant. She flung her bag on the seat beside her as she slid into the booth and pulled out her phone. The brisk air-conditioning cooled her skin and her thoughts.

Val tried to tap out a message, to put into words the conclusion she'd reached during her walk, but thought better of it. She wanted to see him. Talk to him face-to-face, not message him like a twelve-year-old. She decided to call Philip instead and arrange to meet with him. Before the second ring, she heard a chime come from behind her, a sound that brought her out of her booth and onto her feet.

The Philip who stood in a rain-drenched suit at the entrance of Navarro's had to be a product of her overheated imagination.

"That was fast," she blurted out.

"Not really. I tried to get out of there before you left, but they wouldn't stop talking."

Val frowned in confusion, which he noticed instantly. "Oh," he said. "You mean the phone call. I... Okay..."

"I dialed and you appeared." She rushed to the kitchen, scooping up whatever towels she could find before returning to offer them to him. "Here, you're dripping."

He took them, glancing down at his clothes. "Your floor. I'm so—"

"To hell with the floor."

Philip looked up, patting his face dry. "Yeah. To hell with the floor."

Val twisted her hands together, pressing down the longing that had been festering all this time. "I don't like the way we left things back there. It's wrong, after everything, to behave as if we barely know each other. I wanted to apologize for that."

He stepped forward, one towel fluttering onto the

puddle at his feet. "You have nothing to apologize for."

"Yes, yes I do. When you... When we..." She waved her hands in the air, trying to encompass what had happened between them in one gesture. "In our last conversation, you were right. I wasn't seeing you as you were. I've been judging you as if you were somehow your company, and I wasn't taking the measure of you as a person."

"I didn't make things easy for you by lying the way I did."

"Maybe. Obviously, I have issues trusting people. I can blame Luke or I can blame your initial lie, but I'm the one choosing to allow those things to shape my behavior and the way I see you. That's on me."

"You have a right to protect yourself. I don't think my father's actions helped things."

"No, but those were your father's actions. Not yours. You've always had my back." She stepped close to him. The water had stopped dripping from his hair and his nose. "It's why you wouldn't kiss me on our first date. It's why you threw yourself into writing the agreement. It's why you invited me to the fundraiser. You've been trying to do right by me since the beginning. I've been too caught up to see it."

He stepped closer to her until his face was a mere inch from hers. "How can I not, Val? I love you. I will always do right by you."

Val gave a small gasp before winding her arms

around his neck, pressing her warm, dry body against his chill, wet one. "And I love you, too."

His eyes flickered in the dim interior, illuminated by the light that sliced through the windows and across the floor, the rain and wind giving way to a sky as blue as his eyes and as bright as hope. His lips caressed hers, soft and warm and so, so gentle, she wanted to sob from the sweetness of it. His arms were around her and he lifted her off the floor as he kissed her and kissed her and she held on, trusting that he wouldn't let her go.

Epilogue

One year later

Nati had a thing for hummingbirds, an obsession that was born ever since their mother first told them the story of Alida and Taroo, two young people from rival tribes who fell in love. Alida's father discovered their affair and arranged for her to marry a man she didn't love. She prayed to the gods for release, and in response, they turned her into a red flower, the maga flower of Puerto Rico that Val loved so much. Taroo, who did not know why Alida disappeared, waited for her at their rendezvous point in the forest, hoping she would return. After many nights, the moon took pity on him and told him of Alida's fate. He begged the gods to help him find her and, moved by compassion, they turned him into a hummingbird, destined to alight on every red flower in search of his love.

For Nati's graduation party, Val had scoured the internet to find hummingbird-themed place settings and decorations. Failing to find what she wanted, Philip had spoken to Étienne, who got in touch with a colleague who had a friend who had a connection with a party planner somewhere in Southern California. They ended up sending her a box of linen table settings, woven streamers and painted banners with the most delicately designed hummingbirds she'd ever seen. The cost must have been prohibitive, but Val never found out, because Philip hadn't allowed her to get anywhere near an invoice.

"Un regalo, mi amor."

"And I have no choice but to accept this gift, do I?"

"Nope. It's what boyfriends do for their girlfriends. They give them things."

Val's shoulders slumped in mock defeat. She was getting better at accepting Philip's extravagances, but only just. "Only because it's for Nati."

He bedazzled her again with his smile before hauling the oversize box into a corner until it could be transported to Aguardiente in time for the festivities.

Val made to go into their kitchen to make a quick dinner, but Philip caught her hand and led her to the middle of the living room.

"What do you have in mind?"

He shrugged, his face a mockery of innocence. Val knew better than to trust him. She especially didn't trust him when he set his phone on the docking station, and the opening of "Vivir lo Nuestro," the salsa ballad they'd been working on in advance of the party, streamed into the room. It had been a struggle, but Philip had dramatically improved his dancing in the year they'd been practicing together.

He took her left hand in his right one, assuming the perfect lead position. *"Baila conmigo."* His words caressed her ear like a sea breeze.

She stepped into his ready embrace and followed as he went through the seven basic salsa steps. With the gentle pressure of his hand on her hip, he spun her into a nearly flawless turn. Val laughed when he pulled her out of it and they resumed their rhythm.

"I have something for you."

"Philip…no more gifts."

"Shh…" He paused to pull something from his pocket.

When he held out the small red box crowned with the telltale Cartier gold embellishment on the lid, Val quipped, "They do say you're rich." But her voice was shaking.

"I need to live up to that reputation." Soon after the City Hall meeting a year earlier, Andreas had formalized Philip's promotion from head of project design to COO and made his number two status official, paving the way to inherit the company. Val would always be a little sore about the difficulties Andreas had caused her and her family, but their relationship was slowly warming up. She had a far better rapport with Philip's mother, who more than made up her husband's shortcomings.

Philip lifted the lid and showed her what rested inside—a single, classic, rather large solitaire diamond set in a white gold mount.

"*Dios mío*, Philip. The diamond is as big as your knuckle."

His fingers trembled as he took the ring from its cushion. Val blinked away tears to admire its simple design. He knew by now exactly what she liked.

"I thought of planning an event around giving it to you, but I was afraid if I took you to the Eiffel Tower and proposed there, you might take off your shoe and accuse me of being extravagant."

"Propose?" Val was starting to get lightheaded and had to remind herself that fainting would be a terrible thing to do in such a moment.

He held the ring between them. "Val, would you do me the honor of marrying me? Stay by my side for the rest of our lives?"

As if there could be any doubts about her answer.

She held out her hand and let him slide the ring over her finger. *"Sí."*

Ring in place, he captured her hand and kissed it. "I promise to make it good for you."

"You always make it good. Right now. This life we live. Every minute I spend with you." She twined her arms around his neck, leaving small kisses along his jaw and cheeks. He nuzzled into her, reminding her of a giant, blond puppy. "I love you. Don't doubt how happy you make me."

"You, too, *mi corazón*," He turned to press his lips into her palm. *"Te amo tanto."*

She pulled him down for a soft kiss. The tender strains of a new ballad tinkled around them like starlight as they slow-danced, two people who had the rest of their lives to harmonize their rhythm.

* * * * *

WE HOPE YOU ENJOYED
THIS BOOK FROM

HARLEQUIN
SPECIAL
EDITION

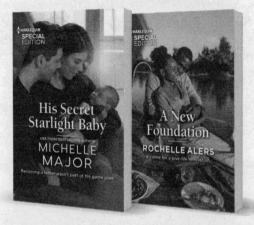

Believe in love. Overcome obstacles. Find happiness.

Relate to finding comfort and strength in the
support of loved ones and enjoy the journey
no matter what life throws your way.

6 NEW BOOKS AVAILABLE EVERY MONTH!

#2863 A RANCHER'S TOUCH
Return to the Double C • by Allison Leigh

Rosalind Pastore is starting over: new town, new career, new lease on life. And when she buys a dog grooming business, she gets a new neighbor in gruff rancher Trace Powell. Does giving in to their feelings mean a chance to heal...or will Ros's old life come back to haunt her?

#2864 GRAND-PRIZE COWBOY
Montana Mavericks: The Real Cowboys of Bronco Heights
by Heatherly Bell

Rancher Boone Dalton has felt like an outsider in Bronco Heights ever since his family moved to town. When a prank lands him a makeover with Sofia Sanchez, he's determined to say "Hell no!" Sofia is planning a life beyond Bronco Heights, and she's not looking for a forever cowboy. But what if her heart is telling her Boone might just be The One?

#2865 HER CHRISTMAS FUTURE
The Parent Portal • by Tara Taylor Quinn

Dr. Olivia Wainwright is the accomplished neonatologist she is today because she never wants another parent to feel the loss that she did. Her marriage never recovered, but one night with her ex-husband, Martin, leaves her fighting to save a pregnancy she never thought possible. Can Olivia and Martin heal the past and find family with this unexpected Christmas blessing?

#2866 THE LIGHTS ON KNOCKBRIDGE LANE
Garnet Run • by Roan Parrish

Raising a family was always Adam Mills' dream, although solo parenting and moving back to tiny Garnet Run certainly were not. Adam is doing his best to give his daughter the life she deserves—including accepting help from their new, reclusive neighbor Wes Mobray to fulfill her Christmas wish...

#2867 A CHILD'S CHRISTMAS WISH
Home to Oak Hollow • by Makenna Lee

Eric McKnight's only priority is his disabled daughter's happiness. Her temporary nanny, Jenny Winslet, is eager to help make Lilly's Christmas wishes come true. She'll even teach grinchy Eric how to do the season right! It isn't long before visions of family dance in Eric's head. But when Jenny leaves them for New York City... there's still one Christmas wish he has yet to fulfill.

#2868 RECIPE FOR A HOMECOMING
The Stirling Ranch • by Sabrina York

To heal from her abusive marriage, Veronica James returns to her grandmother's bookshop. But she has to steel her heart against the charms of her first love, rancher Mark Stirling. He's never stopped longing for a second chance with the girl who got away—but when their "friends with benefits" deal reveals emotions that run deep, Mark is determined to convince Veronica that they're the perfect blend.

Get 4 FREE REWARDS!

We'll send you 2 FREE Books plus 2 FREE Mystery Gifts.

Harlequin Special Edition books relate to finding comfort and strength in the support of loved ones and enjoying the journey no matter what life throws your way.

FREE Value Over $20

YES! Please send me 2 FREE Harlequin Special Edition novels and my 2 FREE gifts (gifts are worth about $10 retail). After receiving them, if I don't wish to receive any more books, I can return the shipping statement marked "cancel." If I don't cancel, I will receive 6 brand-new novels every month and be billed just $4.99 per book in the U.S. or $5.74 per book in Canada. That's a savings of at least 12% off the cover price! It's quite a bargain! Shipping and handling is just 50¢ per book in the U.S. and $1.25 per book in Canada.* I understand that accepting the 2 free books and gifts places me under no obligation to buy anything. I can always return a shipment and cancel at any time. The free books and gifts are mine to keep no matter what I decide.

235/335 HDN GNMP

Name (please print)

Address   Apt. #

City   State/Province   Zip/Postal Code

Email: Please check this box ☐ if you would like to receive newsletters and promotional emails from Harlequin Enterprises ULC and its affiliates. You can unsubscribe anytime.

Mail to the **Harlequin Reader Service:**
IN U.S.A.: P.O. Box 1341, Buffalo, NY 14240-8531
IN CANADA: P.O. Box 603, Fort Erie, Ontario L2A 5X3

Want to try 2 free books from another series? Call 1-800-873-8635 or visit www.ReaderService.com.

*Terms and prices subject to change without notice. Prices do not include sales taxes, which will be charged (if applicable) based on your state or country of residence. Canadian residents will be charged applicable taxes. Offer not valid in Quebec. This offer is limited to one order per household. Books received may not be as shown. Not valid for current subscribers to Harlequin Special Edition books. All orders subject to approval. Credit or debit balances in a customer's account(s) may be offset by any other outstanding balance owed by or to the customer. Please allow 4 to 6 weeks for delivery. Offer available while quantities last.

Your Privacy—Your information is being collected by Harlequin Enterprises ULC, operating as Harlequin Reader Service. For a complete summary of the information we collect, how we use this information and to whom it is disclosed, please visit our privacy notice located at corporate.harlequin.com/privacy-notice. From time to time we may also exchange your personal information with reputable third parties. If you wish to opt out of this sharing of your personal information, please visit readerservice.com/consumerschoice or call 1-800-873-8635. **Notice to California Residents**—Under California law, you have specific rights to control and access your data. For more information on these rights and how to exercise them, visit corporate.harlequin.com/california-privacy.

HSE21R2